Investigating Helen

Book One in the Murder by the Bay Mystery Series

By

Benna Bos

©2021 by Benna Bos
Second publication 2021
Flashpoint Publications

FLASHPOINT
PUBLICATIONS

ISBN 978-1-61929-457-8

Cover Design by AcornGraphics

Editors Verda Foster and Nann Dunne

Publisher's Note:

FLASHPOINT
PUBLICATIONS

Acknowledgments

This book was a journey I needed to take, and I owe the path to many. But my thanks have to start with Kelly Aten-Keilen. Without her encouragement, this book might have stayed on my laptop, unseen, for years. It was she who encouraged me to have confidence in my abilities to jump genres, stretch my authorial wings, and take that all important leap. The team at Flashpoint picked me up from there, providing some of the best editing and writing feedback I've had in my career. Because of Patty and Verda, I am ready to take Agnes and her podcast on new adventures. Finally, I have to thank my two life partners for supporting me in everything I do--my spouse and my dog. Love you both!

Dedication

For Kelly Aten-Keilen and Kari Keilen-Aten

Chapter One

Jolie Green was dead.

Agnes slid farther into the fluffy folds of her comforter, her feet coming into contact with Jasper's big body. The eighty-pound mutt grumbled and snorted but didn't move from his spot at the end of the bed. Five in the morning was too early for him, despite the ringing phone that disturbed them both to bring the macabre news.

Agnes hadn't seen Jolie in years, certainly not since she'd married Derek Green and changed her name. But San Francisco wasn't so big a place that a person couldn't keep track of a schoolmate, especially one like Jolie, the stunning wedding planner whose picture occasionally appeared on billboards and magazines.

Agnes didn't go to reunions or participate in meet-ups, even the social media groups that sprang up around their high school. That was a part of her life she'd mostly like to forget. Jolie was an exception to that rule. But their work lives had no reason to bring them together. Agnes wasn't married and had no need for Jolie's services. And while people enjoyed hiring Jolie, most people didn't want to be in touch with someone in Agnes's line of work. But it seemed Jolie had just met that fate.

Agnes squeezed her eyes shut, wondering if the memory of one very fateful day with Jolie was still as vivid as it once was.

Agnes shivered as Jolie slowly closed the door of the she-shed. Unlike Agnes's wide eyes, Jolie's were half-opened, lids fluttering.

"My mom keeps tons of wine in here." Jolie's slow movements suddenly gave way to quick, bouncy spurts. It reminded Agnes of watching butterflies with her dad in the wetland that sat, undeveloped, at the end of their street. The butterflies would sit quietly on a flower or leaf then spring to life without warning, their wings beating so quickly Agnes could scarcely see them.

"So, um, is your mom gonna, ya know, notice?" Agnes rubbed her toe on the thick oval rug that rested between the door and the flower-patterned couch, which was nestled between matching lounge chairs.

Jolie stood at a short bar behind the couch and worked the top of a bottle of wine with a corkscrew, as her long, blonde hair swished back and forth over her back and shoulders. Jolie was sixteen, with a brand-new driver's license, free rein of the house all summer long while her parents were at work, and apparently the knowledge of how to open a bottle of wine.

At fifteen, Agnes felt worlds behind. The giant leap of having her first boyfriend felt monumental when Joe asked her out during the last few weeks of the school year. She'd gone from playing board games with her parents and younger brother on Friday nights to riding in Joe's mom's car with him at the wheel. They would go down to one of his friends' houses so she could watch him play video games.

That's what they'd been doing this sunny afternoon when Jolie popped up from the couch and asked Agnes to come with her. Agnes sat quietly beside Joe on the other end of the long sofa as he battled Jolie's boyfriend, Seth, in some stupid game she had no interest in. So when the tall, pretty girl held out her hand, Agnes didn't hesitate to follow her.

"Sit down." Jolie's commandment was followed by the sound of wine sloshing into a glass.

Agnes plopped down quickly on the couch as if she'd get burned if she didn't move fast enough. Jolie rounded the furniture and navigated her way between the closely set chairs with two long-stemmed wineglasses delicately perched in her hands. Each glass was filled to within a centimeter of the top. Agnes had never tried alcohol before, but she'd seen her mom drink wine plenty of times with her aunt, and they usually filled the glasses about halfway up.

She remembered it clearly because she always thought it was weird. She didn't tell Jolie she was pretty sure she'd done it wrong, though. She just reached up, took one of the glasses, and carefully balanced it in both hands.

She didn't know Jolie that well. The older girl was going to be a junior, like Joe, while Agnes was going into her sophomore year. They didn't have any classes together but had played on the same volleyball team.

Jolie hadn't spoken to Agnes much, except to say hello or tell her she did a nice job at a game. But today, as they sat on the cream-colored couch in Jolie's house staring at one another around the heads of the two boys—who were wholly engrossed in each other and the video game—a connection sparked, something she couldn't quite understand.

"How come I haven't seen you here all summer? Joe's been here practically every day." Jolie took a sip of her wine. Her fingers gripped the stem of the glass, and her pinky finger pointed outward like a pro.

Agnes pressed her knees together and propped her elbows on her thighs to give extra stability for the glass. "I have to babysit my little cousin while our parents are at work. We don't always stay home. Sometimes we go to the museum and stuff. We take the bus because I don't have a license. I have a learner's permit, but I'm not allowed to drive without an adult, like someone who's twenty-one adult, not like Joe because he's only sixteen and it doesn't count. So we take the bus to the museum and the park and stuff. But...so I can't hang out."

Agnes sucked in a breath and looked down at the light-gray rug. Her cheeks burned. Babbling was a lifelong outlet for uncontrollable nerves. Joe was always telling her to knock it off.

Unable to look up, Agnes took a long sip of the red wine. A slight burn and a low acid taste hit the back of her throat. She swallowed back a gag. Then, because she was a "fall off the horse and get back on it" kind of girl, she took another long sip.

"So where's your cousin today?" Jolie gazed at her over the lip of the clear glass. Wine clung to the side in an opaque curtain, distorting the vision of her chin.

"He's at a summer camp this week." Agnes took another drink of wine. The liquid created a weird sensation in her throat.

"All week, huh?" Jolie's eyebrow raised.

Agnes nodded. The fluffy couch moved beneath her when Jolie sat down. Wine sloshed in the glass. Agnes set the wine on the small, thin coffee table centered among the crowded furniture. Her slow and careful movements delayed her return upright on the couch. When she got there, Jolie was close, her own glass mysteriously gone, her face just inches away.

Jolie put her hands on Agnes's thigh. They were warm and soft, her grip just right. Agnes shivered again. "Do you think I'm pretty?" Jolie asked.

"Yes." There was no way to deny it. Piercing blue eyes and smooth skin, barely marred by the marks common to teenagers, were curtained in soft, flowing hair. More a woman than a girl, she had curves starting to push through her slim figure.

Jolie lifted a hand and ran it over Agnes's face, from her forehead to her chin. "I think you're pretty, too."

Agnes's breath caught in her throat. Her lungs squeezed. Her stomach tingled. But she couldn't move—paralyzed in mid inhale—and Jolie leaned over and kissed her.

Several things struck Agnes at once. Jolie's mouth was softer than Joe's. Joe had a permanent chap to his lips, while Jolie had a soft slide, maybe even helped along by lip gloss. Jolie was slow and deliberate in her movements, whereas Joe was always hurried and intense. Agnes liked the way he needed to get to her mouth with such fierceness, but there was something pleasant about this, too. The biggest revelation of all was that the same subtle sensation she really didn't have a name for—the one that climbed into her body when she was in the mood and Joe touched her with his hands or lips—was present now as well.

Jolie pulled her head back and smiled. "Did you like that?"

Agnes nodded. Breath rushed into her lungs again, and

she struggled not to huff too loudly.

"Do you want to do it again?"

There were consequences to something as simple as the tiny bob of her head now. Agnes knew that. She'd thought about it several times since the day she realized she liked the girl in the set of twins in her sixth-grade class as much as she liked the boy.

Jolie waited. Her long lashes, coated in a thick swath of mascara, fluttered over ice-blue eyes. "Do you?"

Agnes nodded.

****

The hard, cold bench created an ungodly angle holding her ass and back in a way that stabbed at every pressure point, but it was the only thing keeping Helen from crumbling to the floor at that moment, so she supposed she should be grateful for it.

"Hi." A soft voice to her right commanded her attention.

Helen whipped her head to the side. Her gaze landed on a stunning brunette in a lavender pantsuit. "Hi." Just that one short syllable came out in a groggy croak. She rubbed her throat and willed the thickness accumulated there from her recent bout with tears to loosen.

"Are you... Do you need anything? Can I help?" the woman asked.

Helen's eyes traveled from her own rubber shoes to her light-blue scrubs, pants wrinkled, shirt askew, cream sweater thrown haphazardly over the whole ensemble. She was such a mess a stranger was trying to intervene. "I'm okay. Thanks for asking. I'm waiting for the detective." She pointed down the hallway.

The woman nodded. "Me, too. Meeting a detective. They never seem to answer my questions, though." She smiled, and the gesture was one of the most radiant things Helen had ever seen. Teeth—perfect except for a small, cute gap between the front two—shone through pink lips punctuated with understated dimples on either side.

"Um. Yes." Helen had no idea what the woman was
talking about. Cops answering questions? That wasn't how
it worked. In the little experience she'd had with them, it
was the cops who asked all the questions. But whether the
woman's words made sense or not, Helen didn't mind the
soothing company. Sitting alone in a police station wasn't
how she'd planned to spend her afternoon. The longer she
sat, the more frightened and alone she felt.

"I'm Agnes Coates." The woman stuck out her hand.

Helen took it, noting how soft it was, in contrast to her
overly washed ones. And so white next to her brown. "I'm
Helen. Helen Nims."

Agnes sat back in the bench, somehow looking far more
relaxed than Helen thought possible on the wooden torture
device. "You've been here awhile?" Agnes asked.

"I have." Helen had completely lost track of the time,
but it had to have been at least an hour since the detective
who'd brought her here in his unmarked police car deposited her on this bench and disappeared into the bowels of the
police station.

"It's been a busy twenty-four hours for SFPD." Agnes
ducked her head for a moment then looked back up and
smiled at Helen.

That smile was really something. Helen tried to return
the gesture, but it felt flat. She felt flat. "I suppose. I
haven't...I don't talk to SFPD very often." The last time
she'd seen the police regularly was during her ER rotation.

"I'm here a lot." Agnes grimaced. "That sounds bad.
See, I work for *True Crime Tonight*. I try to get information
out of the police all the time. It's my job. Today, I'm here to
get some answers about that guy whose wife and boat
disappeared on the same day."

Helen had seen the show, though not this woman. Helen
would have remembered her. She must be one of the min-
ions who did all the real work while the show's two anchors
got all the credit.

Helen figured they were exchanging careers and blurted
out her own. "I'm a heart surgeon."

"Damn," Agnes said. Her eyes traveled up and down

Helen's disheveled person again. "You don't look old enough to be a heart surgeon."

Age wasn't the problem. The way she looked right now, she was pretty sure no one would allow her to wield a scalpel at their most precious organ. "I've been out of my residency for two years. So I'm still a pretty new surgeon."

Talking to a complete stranger about the details of her life was much more her mom's thing than hers. But at this moment, talking about nothing particularly important with a complete stranger broke through Helen's grief, confusion, and fear.

"I'm always a little blown away when I meet people who had to go to school forever. I mean, I talk to attorneys all the time, but somehow...it's different." Agnes made a face.

Helen managed to laugh, her mind jolted at the unexpected expression. "I'm lucky to get to do what I do. Do you like your job?"

Agnes's eyes sparkled. "I do. I get to do all the fun stuff—the research, the digging, the interviews—without having to show my mug on TV very often. I enjoy it."

"I would be terrible at that." Helen pointed to herself. "Nonconfrontational."

That gorgeous smile hit her again. "I don't know the meaning of the word. I guess that's why my last boyfriend dumped me. And my last girlfriend." Agnes grinned as if she hadn't just casually dropped that she was bi.

Maybe it was the stress of the situation or the need to temporarily escape her grief, but Helen was completely intrigued by this stranger. Extroverts were nothing new to her. She frequently found herself attracted to them. But Agnes was like one of those people you only ever saw on shows like *True Crime Tonight*. So completely self-composed they could speak to anyone about anything without fear or embarrassment, something Helen couldn't comprehend. But she never stopped trying. "I guess you have the perfect job then," she said.

"I don't save lives like you."

"I don't know. My...my ex is obsessed with true crime. I've seen plenty, and I happen to know that sometimes people like you do save lives by getting innocent people out of jail. Or catching killers before they can do it again."

Agnes dipped her head, and Helen couldn't be sure but she thought there was a tinge of red on her cheeks. "The detectives do that. And the attorneys. We just push the buttons."

"That's right. You push the buttons." Helen winked at her companion on the bench.

Complex hazel eyes pierced her. "God, you're pretty."

Helen was no stranger to speechlessness. But now, instead of looking away shyly, she merely stared at Agnes, unable to turn away.

"Sorry," Agnes said, not looking the least bit sorry. "I have a mouth that runs away with me. Am I freaking you out?"

Helen managed to shake her head. She wanted to tell the beautiful woman beside her she felt the same way, but she couldn't get the words out. She could tell her what this little diversion from reality meant, or at least she could try. "I...I really appreciate your company right now."

"Having a bad day?" Agnes asked. Then she hit her forehead with her palm. "Stupid question. You're at the police station. Of course you're having a bad day. I'm sorry."

"You keep apologizing, but you don't need to."

Agnes slammed her with that incredible smile again. "Bad habit. Can I do anything to help?"

Helen shook her head, near tears. She needed a million things right now. None of which Agnes could provide, but she was touched by the sentiment.

Agnes's face fell, pity taking over. "Well, um, if there's anything I can do..." She reached into the massive, leather bag beside her and rummaged wildly through its contents. "I'll, um...somewhere I have a card."

During this frenzied search, the tall man in a dark suit who'd driven her here from the hospital arrived. "Dr. Nims."

Helen stood, clutching her small, brown purse in both hands. "Detective Poll."

He held out a large hand. "Thanks for waiting. We're ready for you now."

"Um. One second." Helen turned to Agnes, who looked up from her bag with desperation. Helen reached into the zipper pocket on one side of her own purse and pulled out a card. "Here." She handed it to Agnes.

Helen followed Detective Poll down a long hallway penetrated by bright, fluorescent lights. He swung into a small room, his back providing her guidance. She moved with him as if those broad, cloth-covered shoulders led to her destiny.

The detective settled her into a chair at a small, rectangular table. He sat opposite her, beside a severe-looking woman who had apparently been awaiting their arrival. "This is Detective Hillman. She'll be joining us for this interview." He gestured to the woman beside him.

"Hi," Helen said.

Detective Hillman nodded so quickly Helen thought she might have given herself whiplash. Detective Poll folded his hands together on top of the table between them.

"How did you know Jolie Green?" Detective Poll's eyes crinkled up at the corners, making Helen feel more at ease than she should.

"I was actually wondering how you knew we were connected." With plenty of time to ponder the question, Helen was dying to know the answer.

Detective Hillman's piercing eyes bored into Helen like a diamond drill working through soft rock. "We're asking the questions here."

Detective Poll placed a hand on his partner's upper arm. "It's okay. It's a good question. We looked in her cell phone."

Of course. Jolie's life was recorded in that phone: every appointment, contact, and text message. They would know how often Jolie and Helen saw one another. They would know that they went to dinner, out on hikes, and shared light, flirty banter by text a few times a day.

The idea that there was no hiding their relationship shot up Helen's spine. Her reaction bewildered her. She had no reason not to be open and honest with these detectives. Why the idea of exposing the truth caused such a response was a mystery she didn't have the time or head space to sort out.

"Oh, yes. That makes sense. Yes, we were seeing each other."

Detective Hillman leaned forward, her elbows splayed on the table. "What was the exact nature of your relationship?"

Helen looked to Poll for help, but he just gazed back at her, head tipped slightly.

"We were dating." Helen didn't have a thesaurus on her so she wasn't sure how many more ways she could put it.

Apparently, Detective Hillman decided to get straight to the point. "Were you having sex?"

"Yes." Helen felt the heat rise in her cheeks. She shared her sex life with a small and elite list of people, if two people could even be called a list. Discussing it with strangers in a police interview room didn't fit into her comfort zone.

Unfazed, Detective Hillman pressed further. "How long?"

"Um. About two months."

"She was cheating on her husband with you?"

Helen shook her head and opened her mouth to defend herself and Jolie against charges of adultery. But Poll beat her to it. "No. Jolie's divorce was finalized nearly four months ago."

Hillman nodded as if this was merely consequential and moved on to the next overly personal question. "Was it serious?"

"Not yet. No."

Hillman stared into Helen's eyes. Her pupils vibrated back and forth as they examined her. The examination had Helen squirming in her rock-hard chair. "So. Not yet means what, exactly?"

Helen shrugged. This difficult conversation needed to push through to more. Confused, shocked, and with the beginnings of grief blossoming in her chest, she needed answers. "We were still in the beginnings of the relationship. Can you tell me what's going on?"

In the most annoying move possible, Hillman answered that question with another. "What do you know about the death of Jolie Green?"

Helen shifted her gaze back to Poll. "Just what you told me at the hospital." Helen couldn't bring herself to relive that moment. She counted on Detective Poll to remember his own words.

Detective Poll nodded. Detective Hillman's stare bored into Helen like it was hard-rock mining for gold. "Do you know how she died?"

"No. I tried to call her mom while I was out in the waiting room. But I didn't get an answer. It doesn't make any sense to me. As far as I know, she was in good health." Helen's chest closed up again like it had at the hospital a couple hours ago when she'd first spoken to the detective.

Detective Poll leaned forward, the audible creak of his chair foreboding. "She was murdered."

The word hung in the air like the sword of Damocles.

Murdered.

Chapter Two

"People are crazy. I can't believe they killed the wedding planner."

Helen swatted Malcolm's chest. As it always did, his hard pecs stung her delicate surgeon's hand. "Be serious."

He frowned at her. "I'm sorry."

In truth, Malcolm's desire to always make her smile or laugh, even in the worst of times, was one of the reasons she found his presence so comforting. Not everyone would spend as much time with their ex-husband as Helen did, something her friends and family often pointed out to her. But Malcolm, despite his inability to be her happily-ever-after, was in fact her best friend, and she needed him now more than ever.

"I just don't understand. I mean, she's a nice lady. She was actually our wedding planner," he told Veronica. "That's how Helen met her."

Veronica Turner was one of the best defense attorneys in the San Fransicso Bay Area. She also happened to be Malcolm's cousin. That's why she was sitting in Helen's kitchen across from her, a glass of wine resting in one well-manicured hand.

"So you and Jolie were friends?" Veronica asked.

Helen exchanged a look with Malcolm. Even though they'd known each other for about six years, Veronica didn't have a clue what she was about to hear next. Malcolm had promised Helen that Veronica would be cool about it.

"We were dating," Helen said.

Veronica took a minute, as people usually did when they first discovered someone they knew was queer. When she did speak, her words weren't what Helen expected. "I thought Jolie was married."

Of course, the old family attitude. They were die-hard

anti-cheating. The entire clan was hard-nosed about it. Before Helen could defend herself, Malcolm did it for her. "Hey, she's not a cheat. Jolie was divorced."

"I never heard that," Veronica said.

"It was kinda on the down low," Helen explained. "She thought the divorced wedding planner was a bad look. And her ex tried to get a big chunk of her money in the divorce, which made it really messy. Anyway, I promise, she was divorced. Our first date was after the papers were signed."

This explanation still didn't appease Veronica. "I saw Derek Green on the news yesterday calling her his wife."

"Yeah," Malcolm said. "He's a problem. That's what we need to talk to you about."

Veronica sat back in the vintage vinyl chair Helen had scored at her favorite antique shop. She took a dainty sip of wine, set her glass down on the Amish-made table, and trained her gaze on Helen. "Okay. Tell me everything."

"Like Malcolm said, Jolie and I met when she planned our wedding. We became friends. We stayed in touch, and we'd go out with groups and friends, sometimes meet for lunch, that kind of thing. During her divorce, she was having a really hard time. And she and I became very close. But, we didn't...do anything until after it was...well, like I said."

Veronica's gaze didn't waver from Helen's face. "So you're a lesbian? That explains a lot."

"No." It was all Helen said. She was tired of explaining. She planned to, but she needed to take another moment to muster the strength first.

During her pause, Malcolm took over. "She's bi, Veronica. And her sexuality didn't have anything to do with our divorce." He sounded just as exhausted about having to go over this again as Helen did.

"Okay. So, you and she started dating. How long ago was this?" Veronica asked.

"About two months," Helen said.

"Was it serious?"

Helen shrugged. The detectives had asked her the same thing. She just wasn't sure. She and Jolie had fun together. The friendship was good. The sex was great. But something was missing, just as it had been in her marriage with Malcolm. Helen had wondered if over time things would change. Now she'd never know. "I guess I'd say not yet."

"Were either of you dating other people?" Veronica asked.

"I wasn't. I can't say for sure about Jolie."

"So someone strangled her while she took a bath, and the police brought you downtown."

"Yes." Tears crept up again as Helen remembered all that happened in that small, blurry, whirlwind of time. Finding out that Jolie had fought for her life: much of the water expelled from the tub in her thrashing, the bruises, the bloodshot eyes. All so vivid and awful.

"Tell me about the interview." Veronica pulled a tablet from the purse she'd hung on the corner of her chair.

"I wish I'd been there," Malcolm said. "Or that I'd known it was happening, so Veronica could be there."

Helen shook her head at Malcolm, her consummate protector. "I didn't realize..." She nearly choked on the words and stopped herself. "It doesn't matter now."

"Well, I wish I'd been there, too," Veronica said. "How many times have you heard me tell everyone in the family: memorize these words—I want an attorney? And there you were, in a police interview room, and you forgot them."

Helen tried to apologize, but Veronica held her hand up. "Just tell me everything that happened. Don't leave anything out."

Helen ran a hand through her short hair. She liked it cut this way, so much less work and easy to keep out of the way at the hospital. She remembered Jolie stroking it and saying how soft it was. "Um. They told me how she died." Helen couldn't bring herself to say "murdered." "And they asked me where I was that night."

"Holy shit," Malcolm said. "They asked for an alibi just like that?"

"Yes."

Veronica shook her head. "That would have been a good time to ask for an attorney."

"Back off, Veronica," Malcolm said. "She's a heart

surgeon, not a lifelong criminal. She probably didn't even consider they were seeing her as a suspect."

Helen swallowed the lump in her throat. Her upbringing was good. In her life there were rough times—being one of a handful of black women in med school, standing out among those—but none of it prepared her for a police interrogation.

"Okay, so what did you tell them about where you were that night?" Veronica asked.

"I was at the hospital doing charts when...when it happened. I'd had a full day of surgery, and I was there late finishing up paperwork."

"I can attest to the fact that's a common occurrence," Malcolm said.

"And people saw you at the hospital?" Veronica asked.

"Yes." Helen reached for her own glass of wine, so far untouched, and gripped it tightly. "I gave them names." She didn't have to work the next day. Everything sucked, and she was constantly on the verge of tears. So she took a long swig of the wine.

"Good. Good." Veronica took notes on her tablet. "And they wrote down the names, I presume?"

"Yes. They did."

"Okay. What else? Did they know the nature of your relationship with Jolie?"

Helen couldn't stop the slight headshake that overtook her. That was the wording the detective had used "the nature of your relationship." As a person who was constantly being told she sounded overly clinical, Helen found it amusing that attorneys and cops had their own clinical ways to say simple things like "girlfriend" or "lover."

"They already knew."

Veronica's head snapped up from her tablet. "How did they know?"

"Jolie's cell phone."

"So they definitely knew you were dating?" Veronica asked.

Helen winced, remembering Detective Hillman's blunt question. "Yes. They knew."

"And you confirmed that?" Veronica asked.

"Yes." Helen's mind was spinning. Did she do something wrong? You couldn't lie to the police, right? Should she have been more vague? Should she have asked for an attorney?

"Veronica, tell me what you're thinking," Malcolm said.

Veronica pierced Helen with her ice-blue eyes, so similar to Jolie's it nearly knocked Helen off her chair. "I think you're a suspect."

****

Agnes practically fell out of the packed elevator. She stared back as the mirrored doors slid closed and wondered how the remaining eight people had so much room when she'd been pressed up against the cold metal the entire twelve-floor ride.

A voice to her right snapped her head to attention. "You hear?"

Jill, her best work friend and the sharp-witted co-anchor of *True Crime Tonight,* marched toward her looking completely at home balanced on a pair of red heels. Her black dress stretched around her long legs as she walked.

Agnes moved to slide into step beside her, shorter, pantsuit-clad legs working harder. "Hear what?"

"We got a love triangle. Nils is practically frothing at the mouth. You know how much he gets off on love triangles."

Agnes stepped behind Jill for a second as they squeezed through a narrow doorway that separated the lobby from the main workspace. In here, the room widened to reveal open-office-concept desks and chairs peppered with large-screen televisions, whiteboards, and round conference tables.

All the action took place in this room. Research was done. Scripts were drafted, edited, and polished. Clips were cut. Then it was all rolled across the hall, past the elevators, to the studio space where co-hosts, Jill and Kyle, shocked the nation with the latest titillating details of true crime.

"Everybody loves a triangle." Agnes threw her heavy-as-hell handbag on her cluttered desk. It landed on a pile of haphazardly stacked papers, a few of which fluttered to the floor.

"I know, right?" Jill perched on the edge of Agnes's desk.

Agnes filed through the stacks of folders to retrieve her most recent research, a legal pad, and a pen.

"Ladies." Kyle Roth marched past Agnes's desk, his head held high, his voice cold as ice.

Jill rolled her eyes. "That dude is such a douche."

Agnes glared at Kyle's broad back. The two slight wrinkles in his grey suit coat taunted her. She had never been comfortable around Kyle. She wished Jamie had never left to join a national show, prompting Nils to tap the newly retired newsman as Jill's co-anchor. The producers thought Kyle would bring credibility to the show. Agnes thought he brought a bad attitude.

Jill frowned at Agnes's pad of paper and brandished her own mini-tablet. "You know, you're the only person who comes to morning meetings with a freaking paper and pen."

"I like the old-school way. So sue me." With her chosen items tucked between her arm and her chest, Agnes led the way toward the massive conference space at the far end of the room.

"Well, you're weird," Jill said lightly as they took side-by-side seats at the conference table.

Cluttered around the oval, nearly twenty people sat jammed together, chair arms knocking into one another with the slightest movement of their occupants. They all muttered and held low-level conversations with one another as they waited for the one empty chair at the head of the room to be filled.

"Hi, ladies," Heath said from the other side of Jill.

Jill rolled her eyes dramatically and turned away from him.

Agnes snickered but then said "hi" back. Heath was not her favorite person in the world, but he'd never actually done anything harmful to her or anyone else that she knew of. He was just kind of—

"Skeevy," Jill mouthed, her face turned away from Heath so he couldn't see her put-down.

Maybe that was the right word, but Agnes gave her friend a censorious look anyway.

"Good weekend?" Heath asked, apparently still trying to get Jill's attention.

Jill gave up and turned half toward him. "Yeah. It was fine. You?"

Heath launched into a tale about how he had some friends he'd gone to the tech school with over for a barbeque, and they got shitfaced and fought some other people. Fortunately, Nils interrupted the asinine story by taking his place at the head of the table and calling the meeting to order.

Their boss did his usual round robin on current projects, talked about what would be on tonight's show, and then turned—in the most dramatic fashion possible—to new assignments. For Nils, it was almost as if, once the work was done and the story on its way to the screen, he lost interest. Always chasing the new story was what put him at the top of his game and the show second in the ratings for its category in the Bay Area.

"I guess you all heard about the love triangle." Nils's straight, nearly white hair bounced around his ears as he bopped in his seat. "Woman, woman, man. One woman dead." He rubbed his hands together as if he were talking about going to eat at the newest five-star restaurant rather than the brutal slaying of a human being.

But this was no different than any other day. It came with the job, and Agnes loved her job. She just had to quash her sense of humanity every now and again. But the words of that gorgeous stranger she'd spent a few special moments with the day before echoed through her brain. They did help sometimes, didn't they? Agnes hoped so.

"So the gal was married, right? And she had a lover...a female lover." Nils's straw-colored eyebrows rose above his hairline. "A freaking heart surgeon!"

Agnes's head snapped back as her attention landed full force on Nils's words. The person she was just thinking of—the beautiful, upset woman she met at the police station—had said she was a heart surgeon.

"Apparently, the woman divorced her husband, then she fooled around with the heart surgeon, then she ended up dead in the bathtub. And the dead woman is no other than Jolie Green, the hot, blonde, wedding planner from the billboards." Nils face was so filled with glee he looked like he'd just won the lottery.

Agnes's heart thumped wildly. Not only was Nils talking about Jolie's death, but he was also saying that the intriguing woman Agnes was so deeply drawn to yesterday had something to do with it. What were the odds?

"Agnes, I'd like you to do the initial research on this story. This has the potential to be big, so throw everything you have into it, okay?" Nils pointed his finger in her direction. Every eye turned on her.

The silence was deep and long as Nils waited for something—a nod of her head, a verbal acquiescence, something, anything. It didn't take too long for him to tire of waiting and move on. He was two words into his next diatribe when Agnes burst out.

"Wait! I can't do the story about Jolie Green."

"Why not?" Nils asked.

If they'd been in a field rather than the middle of a skyscraper in downtown San Francisco, she would have heard crickets. Agnes swallowed, hard. Not usually at a loss for words, her tongue moved around her mouth in a circle, trying to gather any available moisture. "I, um, had a...thing...with Jolie once," she finally said.

Again, total silence filled the room. Like a balloon being pumped full of helium, it was only a matter of time until it burst.

"No kidding?" Nils practically squeaked when he spoke.

Agnes's sexuality didn't usually come up in work settings. But she'd been at the show for five years, from when she was a young intern still finishing college. People had seen her with boyfriends and girlfriends. She didn't think this should be as big a surprise as it seemed to be. "Um, yeah. I date women."

"Yeah, I know," Nils said. "But you dated *her*."

Agnes was pretty sure she should be offended by the way he said it. But she didn't have time for that now. "Yeah. Kind of. A long time ago. So I can't be assigned the case. You'll have to give it to someone else." She looked around the room at Trevor, Olivia, and Sara. None of them moved or raised a hand. None of them even blinked.

The stillness of the room was rocked by Nils clapping his hands together, creating a wave of sound that penetrated Agnes's fog. She jumped in her seat. "That's great!" Nils said. "Oh my God! That's perfect!"

"Wait. What?"

"You"—Nils pointed at her as if he were Uncle Sam on a recruitment poster—"are not only going to do the research for the story. You're doing a podcast, too."

"Wait. What?" Broken record or not, Agnes couldn't stop herself.

"Heath, you'll work with Agnes. Get all the interviews on video and create the podcast. This is your only assignment. Both of you. Go get it!"

Before she could gather her thoughts to protest, Nils was onto the next topic, his hands and words flying so fast it would be impossible to interrupt. After another half-hour of rumination as the meeting wrapped up, Agnes had a whole speech planned for him.

She rose when he did and followed him out of the room, right on his heels. "Nils, Nils. We have to talk."

He was in the doorway of his office when he finally turned. His Scandinavian eyes pierced her. "What is it, Agnes?"

"I don't think I'm the right person to work on this story." Her body slumped as if deflated from getting the words out. One-on-one, surely Nils would see that he had to pivot. He could change the assignment quietly and not lose face. Agnes prayed for it.

Nils turned farther, so his tall, lean body faced her shorter one completely. "I disagree. I think you're the perfect person for this job. You have a personal connection. Not only that, your connection is on the LGBTQ side of this story. That means you can protect that part of the story."

Agnes was floored. She hadn't thought about that for a moment. "What do you mean?"

Nils leaned against the doorjamb casually. "The other shows covering this story are all going to cross the line at some point. I guarantee it. They're going to say something misogynistic, homophobic, *something*. But you won't let that happen. You can handle this case with the grace of a person who's been there but who also sees the victim as a real person. I think your heart is going to make this story better than any other we've ever covered. I can't wait to see what you can do." He chucked her chin, walked into his office, and closed the door behind him.

Agnes slowly made her way back to her desk, mind in a jumbled daze. As much as she wanted to argue against Nils, she couldn't. His point made more sense and had more merit than any other words she'd ever heard him utter. Yes, Nils was a proud-and-out gay man. But he'd never shown the kind of commitment to the cause he'd expressed just now. And Agnes suspected he wouldn't admit to it if anyone asked. Nils had just betrayed his carefully crafted image of a hard-nosed newsman.

In the face of his words—that deep truth about who they both were and what it meant to them deep down inside—she had nothing to counter him with. So she plunked down on the stiff, rolling chair at her desk and resigned herself to her new assignment.

Chapter Three

The bathwater swirled around in a circle; thick bubbles slowed its journey toward the drain. Helen watched her warm bath leave the tub. She sat on the hard porcelain and ran a hand through her wet hair.

Long days at the hospital had never bothered her. Bone weary with muscles made of spaghetti and eyes so sore and raw she could barely keep them open was usually soothed pretty well by a hot bath and a good sleep.

But not tonight.

Her mind wouldn't stop spinning in circles, enhancing her exhaustion without the comfort of knowing sleep was near. Instead, she felt as if her brain would never stop long enough for any rest.

Jolie was murdered. Helen had an attorney. The police wanted to talk more with her. The entire situation was surreal.

The ringing cell phone snapped her out of her thought tornado. She rose quickly from the tub, threw on her terry-cloth robe, and stumbled into the hallway, nearly tripping over Kimber. She scooped her up and grabbed at the phone that sat precariously on the edge of the kitchen counter.

"Hello?"

"Hi, Dr. Nims?"

"Yes?"

"I'm Agnes Coates. Do you remember we met at the police station? You gave me your card."

Helen dropped onto the couch and let Kimber make a nest on her lap. The senior teacup poodle sniffed, scratched, and finally settled. "Yes. I remember. Um, call me Helen." How could she forget the stunning woman who'd given her a break from life that terrible afternoon?

"So, Helen, I'm calling to ask you for an interview." Agnes sounded apologetic.

The television show? That's why a beautiful woman had called her? If that didn't speak to Helen's changing reality, she didn't know what did. "Oh, um, I have an attorney. You need to talk to her."

"And she'll say, 'no comment.' I've been there before. Can we just talk about the possibility? Say over coffee? No tape recorder or anything, I swear."

"I don't think doing any kind of television stuff is my thing." Helen willed herself to hang up the phone, but the part of her that was completely intrigued by the woman she'd met a few days ago stopped her. Not often did people throw themselves out there like a life raft to someone sitting alone in anguish. Most folks, herself included, might get a knot in their chest at the sight of unfiltered pain in the face of a stranger but would feel powerless to help.

This woman was different. While sitting in that waiting room, Agnes couldn't have known Helen would be part of a story she would end up covering. No ulterior motives pressed her to speak to Helen that day and bring a light into a dark place with her random act of kindness.

Agnes pressed on. She touched on Helen's thoughts as if she'd heard them. "Can we just talk about it? I didn't realize. When I met you...I knew Jolie."

The breath Helen sucked in was audible. "You did?"

"We went to the same high school, and one day we kissed. It's...I don't know. She was an important part of my self-awareness even if she never knew it. And then I got assigned to work on the case, and it's all pretty screwed up. I'm sorry to even have to make this call. But my boss convinced me that I'm the best person to work on this story. So will you give me a chance?"

Helen chewed on her lip. Agnes's ramble was adorable, vulnerable, and so convincing. "You wanna meet for coffee? Just coffee?"

"Yes. Just coffee. I swear."

"No cameras?"

"None. I promise."

"Okay."

After they'd made the arrangements to meet the next

morning before Helen's shift at the hospital, she slumped down in her couch, phone still in hand, and wondered what the hell she'd just agreed to. She also wondered how much her acquiescence had been affected by her memory of that long brown hair drifting over a smooth neck and big hazel eyes roaming her body.

The ringing phone once again interrupted her thoughts. This time it was easy to answer and put on speaker, her hand still resting on the couch beside her. With the other, she stroked Kimber's curly hair. "Hi, Mom."

"Hi, sweetie. How are you?" The blatant pity in her mother's voice brought Helen back to earth. No matter how cute the woman was who'd called her a few minutes ago, she'd called for a reason—because Helen's life was in a free-fall.

"I'm okay, Mom."

"No, you're not okay. Tell me how today was."

Helen let out a deep breath. "I was super busy at work. No one asked about Jolie except..." Helen trailed off, realizing too late she shouldn't mention this little tidbit about her day to her mother.

But the damage was done. "Except who? Except what?"

"The head attorney for the hospital, my boss, and I had a talk today about the Jolie thing," she admitted. The meeting was a surprise until the chief of surgery pulled her into a room where the attorney was and closed the door.

"What did they want?"

"They just wanted to kind of go over the whole thing. Jolie's murder is all over the news, and my name has been linked, and..." Helen had gone over the whole thing with Veronica on the drive home from the hospital, and she was too exhausted by it to continue.

"Were they supportive?"

"Yes, of course." It wasn't really a lie. They'd said some of the things they felt obligated to express—condolences, an ear to talk to, and of course support—but the attorney also made veiled allusions to when and how the hospital might drop her like a hot potato if things went wrong.

"Good. You're the most promising surgeon they have at that dump."

Helen would have laughed if her mood would let her. The best hospital in San Francisco was hardly a dump, and as a young, just-getting-started surgeon not even thirty yet, she wasn't exactly the shining star of the extremely talented staff. "It'll be fine, Mom."

Her mother's tone turned dark and somber. "I heard your name on the news tonight."

"It'll be okay," Helen said again, hoping it was true.

"Whatever you do," her mother warned, "don't do any interviews."

****

Agnes crumpled the small, blue napkin into submission, ensuring it could never resume its original shape. She took another sip of her sugary latte and peered at the door again. She was pretty sure a heart surgeon was the type of the person who was never late, but nearly ten minutes had come and gone since their agreed-upon time.

Over the lip of her cup, Agnes watched the graceful, spritely woman drift through the door. Her head swiveled on her long, sleek neck as she sought Agnes out. Agnes raised her hand to make it easier to spot her at the small, round table in the far corner of the coffee shop.

A radiant smile painted Helen's face when she spotted her, nearly stopping Agnes's heart. A pair of perfect legs carried the woman over to Agnes's little perch. "Hi," Helen said. "I'm just going to get a coffee. I'll be right back."

"Do you think I asked what you like to drink for no reason?" Agnes slid an Americano with cream across the small table.

Helen plopped into the other chair, her mouth open as she stared at the drink. "Thanks."

After taking a sip, she looked up at Agnes. "Really. Thanks. This is perfect. Sorry I'm late."

Agnes shrugged as if she hadn't just spent the last ten minutes obsessing over Helen's whereabouts.

"It happens a lot, unfortunately, usually because of work. I have a big surgery this afternoon, and I called to check on the patient. He had an elevated temp that led to a major discussion with several people...anyway, you don't need to hear all this. Sorry I'm late."

"Actually, I think your job is pretty fascinating."

Helen raised her paper cup. "Right back at you."

"I didn't know why you were at the police station when I saw you there, by the way. I'd heard about Jolie early that morning, but not that she'd been... Well, we didn't know all the details yet."

"Crazy coincidence, huh?" Helen's eyes flicked from Agnes to the opaque, compostable cover of her coffee and back again.

"It was. I'm sorry. Were you close?"

"We were dating, as I'm sure you've heard. Hell, everyone's heard. But it wasn't serious. At least...not yet."

Agnes got the message Helen was sending. She hadn't been sure if Jolie was "the one." Agnes understood the sentiment too well. She'd been there herself many times.

"I'm sorry. This must all be very hard for you," Agnes said.

"You knew her. Can you tell me about that?"

Agnes raised one eyebrow. "And you said you wouldn't be a good reporter."

Helen ducked her head. "I've been wanting to ask that question."

Agnes laughed lightly. She couldn't help it. There was something so deeply charming about Helen. The laugh must have jarred Helen because her back hit the rail of the chair with an audible thump as she registered her surprise. Delicate eyebrows raised.

Rather than try to explain what had caused her inappropriate mirth, Agnes launched into the story of how she and Jolie kissed one day in her mother's she-shed, and it sparked a sexual awakening in Agnes.

Helen listened quietly, her teeth worrying her bottom lip. Her eyes—so big and deep brown Agnes could easily get lost in them—gave away every thought. She was interested. She was understanding. She was empathetic.

When Agnes was done, she sat back and took a long, slow drink of her now lukewarm latte, waiting. She had a million questions to ask Helen. But this wasn't like her average interviews for the show. She had to give in order to take. She'd known that from the moment they set this meeting, and she was prepared.

"So she was your first girl kiss?"

Agnes nodded. Questions danced on her tongue, but she bit them back.

"Mine was Lizzie Truman, eleventh grade. She was the star of the girl's basketball team at my school. I've never been athletic." Helen rolled her eyes, as if this were obvious. "But she was also on the Mathlete team I was the captain of." The pride that spiked in her eyes nearly caused Agnes to pitch out of her chair in a swoon. "We were on a road trip to Danville, and we kissed in the hotel room we were sharing."

"So you're a local?" Agnes asked.

"Yes. I grew up in the Castro. Had two moms, until one died of breast cancer. Couldn't stand to leave, so I went to SFU then UCSF. Now I'm a surgeon who lives in North Beach and visits her mom twice a week."

Agnes sat in silent awe of this beautiful little summary of Helen's life she'd just offered up. She had no desire to speak, only to listen. But she was forced to when Helen asked, "What about you? Where are you from?"

Agnes settled into this concept of giving to get. "I grew up in the Central Valley. But my dad got a job in the city my freshman year. That's how I ended up going to school with Jolie. My parents moved back to Sacramento, but I stayed here. Started the job at the show as an intern while I was still in school at Berkeley."

"Do you miss the valley?"

"Hell no," Agnes said. "I wouldn't give up the city for anything."

Helen laughed, the sound light and sweet. "Somehow, I had a feeling you'd say that."

Agnes took a moment to reflect on that statement. They were fifteen minutes into their second meeting, and already

Helen was expecting certain behaviors from her. What did that mean?

Helen said, "I'm sure you didn't ask to meet to exchange stories."

She broke the light mood. But it was just as well. Agnes was here to do a job, not to be completely taken with her research subject. "I want to talk about a podcast."

Helen moved back. "A podcast? I thought this was about an interview for your show."

"That, too," Agnes admitted. "But that would be later on. Right now I want to talk about a podcast."

"About Jolie's murder?"

"Yes. I won't interview only you. I'll interview as many other key players as I can. But your participation would be really important. That's why I'm coming to you first."

Helen sighed. "We didn't date that long. Two months, tops. It only started after she divorced Derek. I don't think—"

"Your story is important. I know it is. I can feel it."

Helen dropped her gaze, pursed her lips, and made an unmistakable "you must be kidding with this shit" face.

"Sorry."

"I get it. You want my story. It's just...It's still all pretty raw, you know? I have a hard time accepting she's gone. And murdered. I just don't understand it all. I don't know how I can..." She ran a long-fingered hand down her neck. "I don't think I'll make a good interviewee."

"I know this is hard. And I'm not just saying that. I lost my college girlfriend. Car accident. I promise to go slow. Hell, talking about it might even help. It did for me." Agnes never meant to share all of this. It was completely genuine, but it was also something she held close to her chest. This give-and-take thing was going too far.

Helen pierced her with those intense dark eyes. Then her entire body relaxed. "Thanks for sharing that."

Agnes's return smile was the most genuine gesture she'd made in years.

"I'll think about it. I have to talk to my attorney. See what she says."

"Yeah. Of course." Agnes reached into her purse. This time she managed to locate her card quickly. She pulled it out and handed it to Helen. "You probably have my number on your phone from when I called you. But, um, this has all my contact information."

Helen took the card gently and didn't touch any part of Agnes's hand. Agnes tried to ignore her disappointment. But when Helen looked at her and said, "I'll be in touch," it changed everything.

****

Helen was right back where she started a week ago. She sat across a scarred, wooden table from the kindly Detective Poll and the stern-faced Detective Hillman. Only this time Veronica sat by her side.

"I don't know what else I can tell you," Helen said.

Veronica put her hand over Helen's. "You don't have to tell them anything."

Detective Poll sighed like a man who'd heard those words more times than he could count. "We didn't actually call you in here today to ask more questions."

"Oh." Helen's entire body tightened from her toes to her scalp. She searched Detective Poll's composure. He seemed relaxed. Her eyes shifted to Detective Hillman, whose rigid posture was no different than it had ever been. "Am I..." Her voice cracked, but she forced herself to get out the words. "Am I being arrested?"

Detective Hillman leaned over the table, her eyebrows forming sharp upside down V's above her cold, robotic stare. "Should we be arresting you?"

Helen's ability to speak completely left her at that point, so she was grateful when Veronica interrupted. "Of course not!"

So subtle it was barely noticeable, Detective Poll moved his hand toward his partner. "No. But we're naming you a person of interest."

"What does that mean?" Helen asked.

Veronica answered her. "It means they get to tell the

media they're looking at someone, and you get dragged over the coals even though they don't have any evidence whatsoever that you were involved."

Helen stared at the side of Veronica's face. "Seriously?"

Veronica's angry glare still focused on the man opposite her. "Yes." Detective Poll didn't deny it.

Helen looked at him. "Can I talk you out of it or prove my innocence or something?" Her rising panic reflected back to her in the pitch of her voice.

Veronica said, "They can do it without any cause. They can ruin your life just because they feel like it."

Detective Poll turned his gaze on Helen. His kind eyes, a deep chocolate brown not that different from her own, were filled with sympathy. "For now, this is just the way it is."

All business, Detective Hillman took over then. "We recommend that you don't talk to any press or give any interviews. We'll make it clear in our statement that you are not a suspect, just a person of interest."

"Sure you will," Veronica said sarcastically. She extracted Helen from the room pretty quickly after that and practically dragged her from the police station. Her grip on Helen's elbow didn't lessen until they were in the little park across the street. She shoved Helen onto a slatted, wooden bench and plopped down beside her.

"Holy shit," Helen said.

"Don't panic. The cops pull this all the time. We just have to play it right."

Helen ran her hand over her hair. She needed to grip onto something real, something concrete in that moment when her life was falling to pieces. "Play? What does that mean?"

"It means we do talk to the press," Veronica said.

Helen's gaze shifted quickly from the well-trimmed grass at her feet to Veronica. "Wait. What? They just said—"

"Forget what they said. They want to create this narrative. We need to take control of it ourselves. Why the hell should we let them run around and imply you're guilty while they attempt to pin a crime you didn't commit on you without finding the real killer?"

"I feel like I'm trapped in a true crime documentary." As soon as the words left her mouth, Agnes's face popped into Helen's head.

Veronica ignored her freak out. Fingers tapping at her chin, eyes scrunched up, she seemed lost in her own thoughts. "We need someone we can trust. Not that those are easy to come by. My clients and I have had a hell of a time finding a sympathetic reporter. Maybe we need to think outside the traditional media box."

Helen tapped Veronica's shoulder to force the intense attorney to meet her gaze.

"What?" Veronica asked.

"I know someone."

Chapter Four

Heath Wiggins. She got stuck with Heath Wiggins. Of all the people to be assigned as her tech person on a gig that was going to require finesse, caution, and careful wording. She had a partner with no filter who—according to Jill—appeared to have grown up under a rock. If there was a stupid question to be asked, she could count on Heath to ask it. If they needed someone to inject with a weirdo conspiracy theory cooked up by someone incapable of critical thinking, she could count on Heath.

"It's hard to believe we've never worked together." Heath slid casually into the passenger seat of the van. "Today's my two-year anniversary at the show, and we've never had a project, me and you."

Agnes fought the battles that mattered. She never bothered to complain about who she was assigned to work with. She'd merely gotten lucky when it came to partners. Tim and Hannah were both incredible techs she frequently got to work with. She never worried about who had her back—until now.

"This is a big one." Agnes pulled the van out of the lot and onto the street. They had a twenty minute drive to Helen's house if traffic was what she expected, as little as ten if it was light. Not a lot of time to instill empathy and political correctness into her wingman, but she had to try.

"Kyle says I'm good."

Agnes repressed an eye roll. In her mind, that wasn't an endorsement. "Oh, yeah?"

"He's got a lot of years under his belt in this field."

Agnes shrugged. "I guess."

"No really. He started as an investigator."

"Sure, but he hasn't actually done an investigation in at least twenty years." Kyle was one of those people Agnes thought should be happily retired and living in some resort town in Florida. She couldn't figure out why he was still hanging around.

"Yeah, well, he just wants to work a few more years, ya know."

"Hmm. I'd retire."

"Yeah, well, I guess he's got some gambling debts." Heath abruptly changed the subject. "Anyway, I've worked on similar assignments to this one."

Agnes kept her gaze on the road and tamped down her irritation. She remembered the rule of interviewing: listen first. "Oh, yeah?"

"Sure. I've worked several love triangles with Naomi. She's kind of the triangle queen."

It was true. In fact, Agnes had fully expected Nils to assign Naomi to Jolie's murder. She still wished he had. "Any with queer participants?"

"Are you allowed to use that word?" Agnes glanced over at Heath. Brows furrowed, he was full of concern. "When I was in high school, that was bad."

Agnes repressed her laughter as she turned back to focus on the road. "How old are you?" Heath was fit, a well-known runner with marathon ribbons on his desk. He had a full head of hair and great skin. Agnes had always assumed he was early thirties at most.

"Forty-five."

"Holy shit. Really?"

Heath let out a long chuckle. The sound was soothing and happy. Agnes realized she'd never heard him really laugh before. "Maybe I don't know much about being LGBTQ language-perfect, but I know you're not supposed to make people feel old."

"Sorry. You just look so much younger. And you—" She managed to stop herself from saying he acted young, too. But the knowing chuckle he let out told her she needn't bother.

"So...queer. It's okay?"

"Yes. It's the Q."

"Oh, right. Duh. Anyway. Yes. I worked on a couple stories with gay guys at the center of them. Never lesbians, though. To be honest, I don't think I know any lesbians."

Agnes couldn't hold back her smirk.

"An old friend and my cousin are both gay, but...wait. Sorry." He stopped himself in a near choke. "How stupid of me. You're a lesbian. So I guess I do know one."

Agnes shook her head. "I'm bi, just like the woman we're going to meet."

Heath shifted in his seat. The leather around him sounded out the action. He'd moved to face her, his eyes directed at the side of her face, practically penetrating her skin. "Okay. So, explain that to me. If you don't mind, that is."

Agnes took a second to reflect on the fact that she had intended to lead this conversation to this place exactly, and Heath himself had brought them there. She took comfort in the traffic jam she saw up ahead. They were getting close to Helen's house, and this could take some time. "It means a person is attracted to both sexes. Or...rather, all genders. For example—"

"I get the basics," he said flatly. "What I mean is, explain to me what it's like for you. What kind of prejudices do you face? Do you get it from both sides, the straight community and the gay community? Do you actually like women more than men or vice versa, or is it really split down the middle? What's the history of the identity? Is it cohesive, or split up based on who you are dating at the time? Is it different for men than for women?"

Agnes's head spun. These sounded like the questions from a sociology grad student doing a research paper rather than a surfing tech operator from a tiny coastal community who didn't know it was okay to use the word "queer."

"Um..." The traffic had loosened, and she saw the turn off to Helen's street. "I'm not sure we have time to go through all of that right now."

"I should have insisted we have coffee first," Heath said.

Agnes was kicking herself. Heath had tried to get her to leave the office an hour earlier for their appointment with Helen to grab a coffee and talk, but she'd blown him off.

"Yeah, sorry."

She slid the van into a parking space about a block past Helen's regal, brick apartment building, impressed she was able to get a spot so close. She shut off the van and turned in her seat. "I promise to answer all your questions after this interview. We'll get lunch. You might have to remind me of the list again. It was long." Heath's face relaxed a little. "For now, just imagine you were capable of loving someone regardless of their gender."

"I can totally imagine that," he said, face completely serious, brows a straight line over piercing eyes.

"Yeah?"

He let out a breath. "We need to talk about your impression of me, Agnes." Then he wrenched open the door and headed to the back of the van to retrieve his recording equipment.

****

The set-up felt strange. Helen and Veronica sat on the loveseat, both rigid as spikes. Across from them, Agnes perched on the antique chair Helen and her mom bought during a weeklong trip to wine country. The guy Agnes introduced as her partner, Heath, was on the floor, cross-legged in front of the coffee table, with the most comfortable piece of furniture, the couch, at his back. He fiddled with laptops and tablets and microphones, all strewn among coffee cups and small plates peppered with the remnants of cookie crumbs.

Meanwhile, Malcolm paced. He created a track from the far window to the entrance to the kitchen and back again and lightly touched Helen's shoulder each time he passed.

Agnes's complex hazel eyes stayed centered on Helen despite the activity around them. "How did you and Jolie meet?"

"She planned our wedding," Helen said simply.

Agnes scrunched up her forehead, and a lock of silky hair fell into her eye. "Whose wedding?"

Malcolm momentarily paused in his obsessive movement. He pointed between himself and Helen. "Ours."

Agnes sat back in the red-velvet pillow cushioning the wicker chair, eyes wide. "Oh. You're married?"

"Divorced," Helen said. "Malcolm is my best friend."

His big hand gave her shoulder a gentle squeeze. "God-damn right."

Agnes examined the still-pacing Malcolm. "Military?" she asked.

Malcolm scoffed, though Helen could see why anyone would think that. Malcolm was built like a tank, and his scoff was just for show. He had plenty of family who served, and he would have been proud to do so as well if he wasn't legally blind in one eye, not that it stopped him from living any of his other dreams.

"He's a dog trainer," Helen said. "He trains guide dogs and medical service dogs and police dogs."

Agnes's intense gaze landed back on her. "Fascinating. How long were you married?"

"Eight years," Helen said simply, knowing the kind of reaction it would get.

Agnes didn't disappoint. "You're..." She looked down at her tablet. "Twenty-nine, right?"

"We got married the day after high school graduation." Helen waited for the question that always followed that statement; "Were you pregnant?"

But it didn't come, probably because Malcolm interrupted. "I thought this was supposed to be about Jolie."

Knowing his growls were harmless, despite how menacing they might sound, Helen raised her hand to cover the smile forming there. She pretended to yawn.

"So Jolie planned your wedding?" Agnes asked.

Helen rubbed her forehead gingerly with two fingers. "Yes. We were having trouble making decisions." She glanced at Malcolm, who stopped his pacing around the living room long enough to give her a sweet grin. "There was a lot going on with all the families. Anyway, one weekend I told Malcolm we needed a professional. He got online and found Jolie."

Malcolm dropped a little input. "She was less expensive back then."

Helen chuckled, the action unfamiliar and welcome.

"Yes. She was. Anyway. That's how we met her. We kind of stayed in touch after that, you know, just through social media. Her mother got sick, and we texted about medical advice for a while. Then one day we ran into each other at the hospital. She'd brought her husband in to the Emergency Room. It was when she filed for divorce. He apparently stuck his fist through a wall."

This garnered a shocked silence from everyone in the room. The air vibrated with surprise. "Should I not have said that?" Helen nodded at the recording equipment. "I mean, it's hearsay right? I didn't treat him or look at his chart." She glanced over at Veronica for help.

Agnes answered. "We can check it out. Don't worry. That's what we do. We won't put anything on the air that's not checked out."

"All right. Anyway, we started to talk again. She was in a rough place, going through a divorce. And I guess I was a shoulder for her, you know. And I liked her, enjoyed her company. But we were definitely just friends at first. In fact, neither of us came out to the other as bi until one night, about two months after her divorce was finalized." Helen bit her lip. While she might be willing to tell Agnes the story of how, in a drunken haze, she and Jolie kissed and then confessed their attraction, she didn't plan to drag out all that on tape.

As she spoke, Agnes stared directly into Helen's eyes. Helen noticed the way the flecks of color were arranged in her irises, the shape of her eyes themselves. Soft brown eyeliner, impossibly thin, was the only makeup Agnes wore along with mascara. A wise choice, it framed those bright eyes like a master work of art, highlighting their beauty.

"You started dating shortly thereafter?" Agnes asked.

"Yes."

Agnes winked, the action brief and almost indecipherable. "And who knew about your relationship with Jolie?"

Helen snapped out of her internal dialogue about Agnes's eyes. She'd been talking about rote things before, practiced things. Now Agnes was asking harder questions. She needed to be on her game.

Malcolm and Veronica seemed to know it, too. Malcolm leaned over the loveseat, squeezing his broad shoulders between the two women. Veronica sat forward, laptop closed for the moment, gaze intense.

Helen started with the easy ones. "Malcolm and his sister, Kristi."

Agnes nodded. Her expression indicated she was waiting for more.

"Um, a friend I went to med school with, Michael."

"Does he work at the hospital?" Agnes asked.

Helen didn't know where these questions were headed. To her, they didn't seem important, but Veronica and Malcolm were tense as hell, so she figured she should be cautious. She decided to answer carefully, thoughtfully. "No. He works in private practice. Why?"

Agnes ran her hand along her neck. "I guess I was wondering if your coworkers knew you were dating Jolie."

Helen shook her head, which was a great way to rip her gaze from Agnes.

"So, you indicated no." Agnes looked pointedly at Heath and his recording equipment.

"No. I have a good relationship with my coworkers, but we spend a lot of our time talking medicine. My love life never came up."

"Does it now?" The question stunned Helen, and it must have shown because Agnes was quick to clarify. "I mean, we haven't gotten to this yet, and I plan to ask about it in more detail later, but I just wondered how all this has affected your life over the past two weeks."

"Well, so far it hasn't been too bad, but the police—"

Veronica wrapped her hand around Helen's knee. "Fortunately, while Helen's name has been leaked to the media, the coverage of her has been mild. We hope to keep it that way."

"A couple people have asked me about it," Malcolm said. Veronica threw him an irritated look, but he didn't seem to care. "I've been asked about it, and it worries me. I mean, that's why we're doing this, right?" He gestured between the three of them at the loveseat and Agnes and

Heath across from them. "To protect Helen from the wrong things getting out there."

Agnes shifted her gaze from Malcolm back to Helen. "I'm doing this because it was assigned to me at work. But as for my personal goal in doing the podcast, I hope that it will unravel the mystery of Jolie's death, of course. And I would also like it to help the innocent people left behind in the wake of this tragedy."

Helen searched the gold-flecked eyes of the woman across from her, desperate to find answers in them. Did Agnes think Helen was innocent? Did she care?

"Then we have the same goal," Veronica said. "Because Helen is an innocent victim. That brings me to my next question. Who else are you planning to interview for this podcast?"

"I'm going to talk to everyone who will consent. Friends, neighbors, Jolie's family."

"What about Derek?" Malcolm asked.

"I'm already working on it. It might be hard to do. But I'll throw everything I've got at it, call in every favor, and do just about anything to get an interview with Derek. I promise you that," Agnes said.

Despite her inability to read Agnes's mind, Helen believed her.

****

If Agnes could wish away the three other people in the room so she could be alone with Helen, she would. But of course, that wasn't going to happen. Malcolm and Veronica stood like sentries at the gates of the Alamo, willing to lay down their lives to protect Helen. Heath, much to her surprise, remained quiet and unobtrusive during the entire interview. A few times, she'd even forgotten he was there, the sign of a great tech.

Ninety minutes flew by, and Agnes knew she had to wrap up the interview. "There's so much more I want to go over. Can we go ahead and schedule the next session now?"

Helen's graceful expression nearly melted her. "Sure. I

can do this again next week at the same time."

Veronica jumped up from her seat. At first, Agnes thought she was planning to finally answer the phone in her hand, that while silent and still, had been constantly lighting up throughout the interview. But Veronica's attention was seated squarely on Helen. She stood over her, brows knitted. "Perhaps we should discuss this first, you know, debrief, before agreeing to continue."

Agnes put on her best negotiator voice. "Why? Was there a problem with anything that happened today?"

Veronica spun around to stare at her. Her expression was no less severe or unkind than it had been all day. "No. There wasn't. But today was the softball day I'm guessing." She raised one thin eyebrow.

"That's true." Agnes craned her head to see around Veronica, peering at Helen. "It's true. We'll be getting into more emotional territory in the next session, talking about Jolie's death."

"I understand," Helen said. Her steel-infused gaze landed first on Veronica, then Malcolm. "And I wouldn't have agreed to any of this if I wasn't prepared to talk about everything. I'll be fine."

Spouses and former spouses often knew when to push and when not to, at least that had been Agnes's experience during dozens of this type of interview. Malcolm followed suit. He turned away from Helen, and his concern-laced expression softened. He focused on Heath. "Hey, can you show me what you're doing over there?"

Heath looked up from the equipment. "Sure." He patted the section of carpet beside him, and Malcolm quickly folded himself into the spot. The two of them became lost in their own discussion.

Veronica shrugged and pulled her phone to her nose. "I have calls to make." She marched out of the room and down the hall.

Helen's lips formed into a self-satisfied grin as she rose. She reached for the clutter of dishes on the coffee table. "I better pick up."

Agnes jumped up. "Let me help."

Arms full, the two women headed into the large, airy kitchen. Instantly hit with jealousy over such a perfect space, Agnes inhaled sharply as she swung her gaze around the room. "How did you get a kitchen like this?" Two large windows broke up the endless cupboards that were painted an elegant off-white. Classic-looking appliances and a stenciled backsplash complemented more counter space than she had ever dreamed of.

"My mother-in-law is an interior designer. Well, my ex-mother-in-law."

"A good one," Agnes said.

Helen laughed. "Yes. And a rich one." She set the plate of scone crumbs on the counter and took the coffee carafe from Agnes's hands. "Thanks."

"Are you a good cook? Because, I mean, with a kitchen like this you could have your own cooking show."

"I'll stick to surgery. I'm actually not very good at cooking. I never had time all through school and residency, so I never really learned. I do like to bake though. It's sort of my day off Zen thing to do. What about you?"

Agnes leaned against the counter, opposite where Helen stood beside the sink. Light streamed in from a window behind her, making Helen's smooth skin practically glow. "I like it. I cook for friends quite a bit. My grandmother taught me. She was a whiz in the kitchen."

Helen's sweet smile nearly undid Agnes. Her reservations about taking this gig had begun with her fears about her personal connection to Jolie, but she was quickly becoming alarmed at how aware she was of her attraction to Helen.

She cleared her throat and tried to put herself into work mode. "I wanted to tell you how brave I think you are."

"Brave? What did I do that was brave?"

Compelled to be closer, Agnes pushed off the counter at her back and moved toward Helen. The light shifted, and her features came into sharper focus. The dark, liquid eyes, the high cheekbones, the pillowy soft lips. "In the middle of all this, you're telling your story. That's not an easy thing to do."

Helen tipped her head. "Did you ever tell yours, about

the friend who died in the car crash."

"She was much more than a friend," Agnes said. "And no. I tell other people's stories. I'm not brave enough to tell my own."

"You told me about it. I mean, we'd just met, and you told me that it happened. And now you're telling me that it meant a lot to you. That she meant a lot to you."

Agnes let out a breath and with it the truth. "You're easy to talk to."

"So are you. I'm glad it's you doing this thing." Helen paused, but she clearly wasn't done. So Agnes waited. "To be honest, I probably wouldn't have agreed to it if it were anyone else."

Agnes took a step closer. "I feel like I know you."

Helen sucked in a deep breath, the action audible. Her chest rose, and her eyes grew wide. They were so close Agnes felt the breath hit her neck when Helen released it again. "Do you believe in past lives?"

Agnes shook her head.

"Me neither. Worth a try, I guess."

The air hung thick and laden with unsaid things. It was hard to see through it, difficult to speak, and impossible to move.

Veronica's voice shattered the bubble. "Helen, what's your Wi-Fi password?"

Helen slipped to the side and moved away from Agnes at a disturbing speed. She swung open the kitchen doors and disappeared.

Chapter Five

"But the anchorman said it like—"

Helen said, "Mom, I don't want to talk about this anymore. Can't we please just have a nice dinner? This is your favorite restaurant." She gestured around the room. It wasn't high-end, despite her mother's ability to afford it. But Yasmine Nims loved the little local bistro.

"No it isn't," her mother said.

Helen shook one of their famous crusty rolls at her. "What? Yes, it is."

"It used to be. But now my favorite is that new Greek place that opened up near where I get my hair done. And my second favorite is the taco truck on Montgomery. So this is probably my third favorite now," Yasmine explained.

"Fine, third favorite. What are you having tonight?" Helen waved the roll over the menu before sinking her teeth into its crust.

Yasmine leaned forward, her long braids cascading over her shoulders. "Maybe I'll try something new."

Her mother liked to do that, try new things. Every time they went out to eat, she attempted to find something different on the menu. Though at this point, Helen wasn't sure she'd be able to find a new item since they'd been here enough for her mother to have had everything at least once.

Helen, on the other hand, took after her mama. Nancy Smith-Nims was a woman of habit. She had exactly one dish on every menu she would eat. She was adventurous in the kitchen, but when they were out and about, she was "stiff and stuffy" as her mom liked to say.

That sense of variety behind closed doors juxtaposed with careful caution in the outside world extended to other things as well. Nancy had painted each room of their house a different color. But only ever wore black or grey when she went out. And as Yasmine had confessed over Helen's objections, while Nancy wouldn't even hold her wife's hand in public, she'd been a wild woman in bed. Despite not wanting to know a thing about her parents' love life, she kind of liked knowing where that came from.

Of course, Nancy wasn't her biological mother, nor was Jasmine. She'd been adopted at two weeks old. But that never mattered to Helen. She'd never searched for answers to her genetic make-up. Even though as a doctor she understood the role genes had to play in shaping a person, she put much more stock in nurture, at least for herself.

So it was with love and a little bit of exasperation that she watched her mother scour the menu for a single item she hadn't yet tried. "I guess it's a good thing this isn't your favorite restaurant anymore, because it might be the end of an era, here."

"Wait! I found one. I haven't...oh, yes I have."

Helen finished her roll as Yasmine continued her doomed search. Their server approached before her mother could uncover the hidden gem she was so sure was there.

"Do you guys have a special?" Helen asked, quite certain she'd never heard of any at this place before, but grasping at straws so they could order and get on with dinner.

"Hey, you're that lesbian murderer from TV."

The next few minutes were a blur. Yasmine Nims stood so quickly her chair pounded to the floor with a loud clap. Her thorough taking apart of the young waiter drew the attention of every person in the place. Then she hauled Helen up and dragged her from the restaurant. All the while, she promised never to return and reminded them what a good customer she'd been over the years.

Outside, the sounds of cars passing, the occasional horn, and people talking loudly on cell phones as they walked down the sidewalk all failed to penetrate the aching fog Helen was trapped in. This was all so surreal. Just that night she'd been mentioned on the local news again, and now she was being recognized—as a murderer.

Helen hung her head in her hands. Yasmine had one arm around Helen's shoulders while she used the phone with the other. She made a demand to whoever was on the other line. "We need a ride, now."

Helen wanted to protest. Sure, she wasn't entirely in the mood to flag down a cab and keep her shit together through the ride home, and she definitely couldn't keep her mother's temper in check. It would suck for the cabbie, but it was doable.

Yasmine spoke into the phone with speed and authority. "I'll tell you all about it when you get here. Needless to say, I'm about to stick my designer boot up someone's ass."

"Mom. It's okay. We can get a cab."

But it was too late. Yasmine hit the button on her phone with unnecessary force and shoved it in her purse. Her gaze was focused on something. By the time Helen realized the object of Yasmine's attention was a suited man with a gold nameplate who plunged out of the restaurant and was headed their way, her mother was out of reach. Helen grasped at air where Yasmine's arm had been.

Scrambling to keep up, Helen marched toward the restaurant entrance, hot on Yasmine's heels. "Mom. Leave it."

Yasmine, blind and deaf to all but her target, rounded on the man. "Are you the manager?"

The sleek suit, tight lips, and slicked back hair screamed his profession. This man could be walking through a grocery store or a park, and you'd know he was a restaurant manager. "Yes, ma'am. I understand there was an issue?"

"An issue! I'd say there's an issue. I am one of your best customers—"

"Yes, ma'am. I recognize you, and I know you come here frequently."

"I did come here frequently. Not anymore. My daughter is an amazing woman." Yasmine reached blindly behind her and slapped at Helen, reaching the edge of her upper arm. "She is an accomplished surgeon, graduated second in her class. Commands the respect of her colleagues. She's also a sweet and compassionate person. She volunteers her time. She works with foster kids. Do you do anything like that?

She also helps fundraise for the animal shelter. Last year, she co-chaired an event that brought in over two hundred thousand dollars. Do you do things like that?"

Until this moment, Helen had never imagined that she would relive the rich embarrassment of childhood. But now she was in the deepest pit of parental humiliation imaginable. "Mom. Please!"

She may as well not have spoken. Yasmine took her flaying arms out of play by tucking them into her chest in a defiant fold. "Well do you, Mr."—she leaned over and squinted at the shiny nameplate—"Linton?"

Mr. Linton leaned down and wrapped his lips into an ingenuous smile. "This isn't about me. It's about your beautiful daughter. And I would like to offer you both a free meal of your choosing and a bottle of wine on us during your next visit."

"You can take your free bottle of wine and shove it—"

For the first time in her entire life, Helen physically accosted her own mother. She managed to get her hand planted over Yasmine's mouth. The shock actually caused the sputtering mama bear to fall silent. "Thank you very much," she told Mr. Linton. "We're fine. And our ride is here. Have a nice night."

Helen released her mother's mouth and took hold of both her arms, steering her away from the restaurant and toward the curb. Lying about their ride being there was the least of her worries. She turned toward the street as if expecting to see a cab arrive at any moment.

It was a bit of a shock when a familiar SUV pulled up directly in front of them. "Malcolm? You called Malcolm?"

Her mother didn't answer. Instead she wrestled open the back, passenger-side door, leaped in, and scooted across the leather seat to make room for Helen. Helen followed automatically until they were both securely inside the vehicle.

Malcolm turned in the driver's seat to look back at them. "I heard we had an emergency. We were just a few blocks away, so we came right over."

Yasmine didn't bother with pleasant greetings. Nor did

she immediately address the "we" as Helen wanted to. "Thank you. Please take us to Helen's."

A woman in the passenger seat whipped her head around to stare at them.

Helen nearly died. Clearly, this was the other half of we. "Hi," Helen said.

The woman returned the short greeting and stared for a moment longer before looking ahead again.

"Helen, Yasmine, this is Tina. We were on our way to dinner when you called." Malcolm's tone didn't betray the slightest bit of irritation.

"You're on a date?" Helen asked, appalled that they had interrupted. She turned on her mother. "You interrupted his date?"

"It's fine," Malcolm said.

Helen seriously doubted Tina thought it was fine. "I'm so sorry."

"We'll just drop you off and head out from there," Malcolm said. "Right, Tina?"

"Yeah, no problem." She sounded sweet and accommodating. That was good. But no matter how nice Malcolm's date turned out to be, she still shouldn't have to put up with this—his ex-wife and hysterical ex-mother-in-law in the backseat.

Malcolm pulled out into traffic and hit a stoplight almost immediately. He glanced in the rearview mirror. "So, spill."

Helen let out a deep breath. She didn't think her night could get any worse than it already was. But recounting the painful and humiliating incident at the restaurant in front of Malcolm and his date wouldn't help. "It wasn't as bad as Mom made it out to be."

"Bullshit!" Yasmine practically quivered with anger.

"Mom. Please." Her other mother had always been the one to temper Yasmine. With her gone, Yasmine had no filter, and at times like these it became abundantly apparent.

Yasmine ignored her and shot her finger toward Malcolm. "Did you see the local news this morning?"

"No. I'm afraid not." Malcolm's shoulders pressed

against the seat back, but his eyes remained on the road as he took a turn onto Geary.

"I did." The soft voice from the front seat startled Helen. Tina turned around to face Helen and Yasmine. She was a small woman with delicate features and kind eyes. "There was a story about you."

"Wait. What?" Malcolm's tension filled the air.

Helen needed to jump in before this train went off the tracks. "It wasn't that bad. The story wasn't actually about me. It was about Jolie, and my name got mentioned, that's all."

"Sorry. You're right." Tina's naked expression of pity was kind but it did nothing to lighten Helen's mood.

"You were mentioned how?" Malcolm asked.

"I'll tell you how," Yasmine interjected. "They implied that she was some seedy lover on the side."

Malcolm's eyes shot to the rearview mirror again. "It that true?"

Helen focused on the direction of the car rather than the direction this conversation was heading. There was a reason she'd deflected her mother at the restaurant. "Don't miss this turn, Malcolm, or you'll have to go like three blocks to find a two-way road and get back."

Malcolm sighed and pulled the car onto Helen's street. Helen couldn't wait to get into her home, scoop up Kimber, and shut everyone else out. But it wasn't that simple.

"Come on up," Yasmine offered the minute the car stopped at an impossibly convenient place in front of the condo.

Helen stayed silent as all four of them piled out and headed into her home. Kimber wasn't big on strangers, and instead of providing her pet parent with much-needed cuddles, she ran and hid under the bed.

Yasmine, acting as host in her daughter's place, got everyone situated on the furniture and shoved drinks into hands before getting back to the drama at hand. "The news story was about Jolie and her murder. They made it sound like Jolie was married at the time of her death."

"Which she wasn't," Malcolm said.

"No," Yasmine said, "but they seemed to have left out that little detail. Then they mentioned that Dr. Helen Nims had been dating Jolie for months. That's what they said. Not two months or since the divorce. They made it sound so seedy."

Helen put her hand over her mother's wrist. "It wasn't that bad."

"It was, too. Did they even call you before they did the story?"

"No," Helen said.

Malcolm threw his hand up like a Stop sign. "Wait. This isn't the same show that's doing the podcast, is it?"

Helen shook her head vigorously. "No. Definitely not. It was just Channel Four."

Yasmine's indignation could not be quelled. "Well, just Channel Four was enough to get you recognized and verbally assaulted in the restaurant tonight."

Helen hung her head in her hands. Somehow her life had become a circus. Despite the divorce, dating a woman, coming out to friends and colleagues, her life experience had never felt so completely out of control. All of that had been planned and thought out. Every step of her journey in life was under her control, until now.

"What can I do?" Malcolm asked.

Despite being kind and patient, the way Tina's head moved to the side to look at him at that statement was a red flag for Helen. She loved Malcolm, but he wasn't her husband anymore. He'd already been there for her so much through this entire ride through hell she was currently stuck on. But now it was affecting his life.

"The ride home was perfect," Helen said. "Why don't you two go back out and enjoy your evening. That would actually make me happiest at this moment."

Ten minutes later, Helen returned from the door where she'd shown Malcolm and Tina out. Her mother was sprawled on the couch with tightly pressed lips.

"I don't get it." Yasmine held her glass out to Helen, a not-so-subtle hint that she'd like it filled up again. "I don't understand why you and Malcolm got divorced. It's clear as day you love each other."

This conversation was exhausting. If it were anyone else besides her mother, Helen would refuse to hash this out yet again. But when it came to Yasmine, she had no choice, just like she had no choice to wear turtlenecks at Christmas or accompany her mom to church on holidays.

"I do love him. He does love me. We're best friends. More than that even. We're like siblings. That might make us great companions, Mom, but it doesn't make a marriage."

"I just don't buy it."

"What?"

"Nancy was my best friend, my confidante. Don't tell me it's some sex thing, because I know you all had sex. Hence the pregnancy scare when you were in med school, remember?"

Helen ran her hand over her face and let a small groan escape her throat. "Thanks for bringing that up, Mom."

"So, was that it? The sex dried up?"

"Actually, it did," Helen said. "Though that wasn't the sole reason for the divorce. We literally began to treat each other like brother and sister. It was almost weird."

Yasmine huffed. "It's too bad."

"Yes, it is," Helen agreed. Then she echoed a line her mama used to throw at them both when things were tough. "But that's just the way it is."

Yasmine reached out and stroked Helen's face with a soft, motherly touch. "Do you think you'll ever find that spark again, like I had with your mama?"

The image of her and Agnes in the kitchen, tension hanging between them like thick curtains, flashed in her mind. "Yes. I do."

****

Agnes was pretty sure that Cheryl Knight was a researcher's dream come true when Cheryl ushered them through the doorway of her opulent condo on the hill and practically shoved Heath toward the kitchen window. "See there? You can see right into the apartment across the way. See?"

Heath nodded at the short woman with white hair and tiny, wire-rimmed glasses as he nearly tripped on the stepstool she had placed in front of the window. "I see."

Seemingly satisfied with that, the Mrs. Claus look-alike pulled them through each of the three bedrooms, the living room, and even the two bathrooms, giving them a thorough tour. As she moved, Cheryl talked constantly, mostly about her late husband, Hank. "Hank and I purchased this back when people like us could afford to live in a neighborhood overlooking the Bay."

Heath and Agnes followed as Cheryl yanked open a set of French doors and invited them out onto a spacious balcony. She pointed to a set of patio furniture. Agnes and Heath automatically sat on her command. Heath swung his large pack to his side and began setting up his recording equipment.

Cheryl's eyes lit up as she watched Heath, and her voice grew louder. "Hank died four years ago, but we did well with our donut shops. Did I mention we grew them from one to ten in just five years?"

She had, in fact, mentioned it three times already, and Agnes wished she hadn't been counting. Cheryl had also explained in blatant terms that the proceeds from the donut shops had left her with enough money to live out her days surrounded by far richer neighbors.

It was those neighbors that had brought Agnes and Heath here. It seemed that Cheryl spent a lot of her time keeping track of their comings and goings. Two years ago, when Derek and Jolie Green moved in next door, she was no less attentive to their antics. "Those kids fought all the time. Constantly yelling and screaming at each other."

Agnes's heart clenched. She hated to think of Jolie in an abusive relationship. "Did they get physical?"

"Oh no. It wasn't like that. They were both just quick tempered and hardheaded. I've had more neighbors like that than not. I just notice because Hank and I never raised our voices, not once in thirty-eight years." Cheryl held her head up, stretching her neck. She reminded Agnes of a bird preening.

Heath shuffled onto the floppy cushion beside Agnes. They were seated on a wicker bench perched to one side of Cheryl's rectangular balcony. Agnes's back was to the bay, which was good, because the incredible view would have distracted her from the woman sitting stiffly in the matching chair opposite them.

"So, um, nothing too unusual about their relationship then?"

"No. They were all right, I guess. They didn't have other lovers in and out of there like the Thompkins couple. I swear they're swingers. But you know, they say Jolie Green walked on both sides of the track. Though I never saw that. So if she did, she kept it under wraps."

Agnes didn't think any discussion of sexuality was a path she wanted to take with Cheryl. So she moved along. "I understand they divorced not too long ago."

"Oh yeah, Jolie made sure to tell everyone she could that she was divorced from Derek now. But he still came around all the time. I heard her schedule a locksmith to come change the locks the day before her death. But obviously he didn't show up, since Derek was at the condo the next night. He supposedly has some bachelor pad in the Mission. But he was always here."

"And he was here the night Jolie was killed? Can you tell me about that night?"

Cheryl leaned forward. "Oh I can, all right. I'll tell you everything I told the cops, and I'll give you one better."

"One better?" Agnes glanced at Heath. He in turn gazed at her with wide eyes. Were they about to get a scoop even the police didn't have?

Cheryl nodded at her enthusiastically. A lock of spiral hair, colored in a swirl of salt and pepper, fell over one eye. "I drew a picture of the man I saw."

"Okay, wait. Back up. Start from the beginning." Every atom in Agnes's being screamed out to fast-forward to the mystery man, but her reporter's conditioning took over.

"So that night, Jolie came home from work or wherever she'd been." Cheryl threw one hand in the air dramatically. "She was all dressed up, like always. It was late, probably ten o'clock. She came home late a lot, especially on the weekends because of weddings, but this was a Thursday night, so who knows where she'd been. Anyway, I could hear her high heels clicking on the pavement that runs up to the door." Cheryl pointed down to where a path led from the small parking area to the front lobby of the building. From Cheryl's third-floor balcony, she had a perfect view. "And like I showed you, my kitchen window looks out kitty-corner to theirs because of the angle of the building. I happened to need to wash my dishes. So when I heard Jolie come home, I went over to the kitchen window." Cheryl took a pause, staring into first Agnes's eyes then Heath's. The woman was a born storyteller, and she was checking to make sure she still had her audience.

"Was anyone else in the house?" Agnes asked.

"Derek was there. He'd been there for hours. Must have come over right after work. Used the key he still had. I don't know what he does for a living, but he keeps banker's hours, you know. Done at five o'clock sharp every day. I wish Hank had those hours when he was working."

"Did you see anything through the window?" Heath asked. Then he immediately shrunk and looked at Agnes apologetically. She grinned at him and nodded.

"Just shadows. But here's the kicker. I saw three shadows." Cheryl raised one penciled eyebrow.

"Who was the third shadow?" Heath asked. The innocent look on his face, like a kid caught up in a story, was kind of adorable. So Agnes didn't intervene. Despite her training, she felt no overwhelming need to assert control over the interview.

Cheryl threw her hands up and shrugged her shoulders. "I have no idea. I never saw anyone else come into the house. But there were three shadows." She pinched her thumb and forefinger together and brandished the remaining three fingers toward her audience. "Then I couldn't see or hear anything. About half an hour later, I heard the water running in the bathroom—see the pipes go through our adjoining wall. Then nothing for a good twenty minutes. Then I came out here to my balcony. I was having an evening toddy. The weather was real nice. No bugs. And I happened to be looking over at the building entrance."

Cheryl pointed down to the glass doors that could be seen fairly well from the balcony. Agnes had no trouble imagining the woman not only looking over the entrance to the building, but regularly craning her neck to get the best possible view of every person coming and going.

Heath and Agnes leaned forward at the same moment, elbows on knees in misshapen mirrors of one another. "What did you see?" Agnes asked.

"Derek leaving."

Heath scrunched up his brow. "Leaving? So he left Jolie alone with the mystery man?"

Cheryl nodded her head so distinctly, her neck arched back and forth in an almost impossible angle.

"What happened next?" Agnes prompted.

"Nothing for a good long while. At least half an hour. I stayed right here and kept my eyes on that door. But nothing. No one came and went. Then...Then, I saw a man running out of the building at full speed. He left so fast, the door banged closed behind him with a terrible thump, like it does when the teenagers slam it."

"Did you get a good look at him?" Heath asked.

"No, not really. He was moving too fast, and the lights from the building are pointed poorly, so it's hard to see people well at night. I could tell he was tall, though, and wore a baseball hat."

"Which direction did he go?" Agnes asked.

"He took a sharp right, toward the parking lot. I couldn't see him after he rounded that corner." Cheryl pointed to the edge of the building.

"And you think this person had some involvement in Jolie's death?"

"Of course," Cheryl said, as if Agnes were a complete dolt.

"How do you know?" Heath asked.

"Because I'm sure that the man I saw running out of the building was the third man in the condo that night. I know it!"

"Okay. So, what happened after that?" Agnes hoped her calmer voice would settle Cheryl a little so they could get the rest of the story out of her.

It seemed to work. Cheryl leaned into the cushion behind her. "I went to bed. I heard about Jolie when the police knocked on my door at two in the morning."

"Okay. That makes sense because Derek called the police when he got back to the condo at..." Agnes glanced down at the notes she'd been keeping. "One in the morning. So over two hours after the man ran out, right?"

Cheryl pursed her lips, her light pink lipstick flattening out in a hard line. "What's your point?"

"How do you know that man you saw running out killed Jolie?"

Cheryl leaned forward and stared into Agnes's eyes with an intensity Agnes could barely believe was coming out of the flighty woman. "I told you about the bath water running before the man left. And as you know, Jolie was found dead in the bathtub."

"The bath ran before Derek left, too," Heath pointed out.

Cheryl tapped her finger on her lips and squinted her eyes at him.

"But she was strangled, right? Or at least that's the rumor." Agnes pulled Cheryl's attention back to herself with her question. "So couldn't someone have strangled her three hours after she took a bath then put her in the tub? Or couldn't it have been someone else taking a bath when you heard the water running?"

"Like who?" Cheryl practically shouted. "The mystery man?"

Agnes shrugged, but Cheryl blew her off with a wave of her hand.

"I will say this." Cheryl stuck one finger in the air. "I talked to those cops and EMTs when all the hustle and bustle was happening, and I overheard one of them say that the water was cold when they pulled her from the bath."

Agnes narrowed her eyes. "I see. So, if the man killed her then fled, where was Derek during all of this?"

"I heard all about that." Cheryl gave Agnes another hand wave. "He went to the pub down the street. Walked there. Probably where he was headed when I saw him leave. Lots of people saw him there. When he came home, half drunk, she was dead. That third person must have done it."

"Who do you think the third person was?" Heath asked.

"A hitman," Cheryl said with utter confidence.

"Hired by whom?" Agnes asked.

"I heard it was the doctor, you know the one who was getting it on with Jolie."

Agnes nodded sharply and ducked her head to gaze down at her lap. "Is there any proof of that?"

"It all adds up." Cheryl ticked the facts off on her fingers. "The doctor hired the guy. He goes over there and drinks with that Derek. Probably gave him some reason to go to the pub, had a girl waiting or something. Who knows with men like that. Then he kills Jolie and takes off. It all adds up. I'm not stupid. I can put two and two together."

Cheryl's tone indicated she was getting pissy. Agnes couldn't risk not getting to see this secret weapon Cheryl had promised, so she nodded and smiled. "That makes sense."

Cheryl seemed to be satisfied by this. She grinned, and her eyebrows arched high above her eyes. "You want to see the picture now?"

"Yes, please," Agnes said.

Cheryl popped into the house and returned a moment later with a large envelope. She carefully removed her prize as if it were a lost Van Gogh. Her face was filled with pride as she turned the piece of paper over to reveal a pencil sketch of a blurry two-legged figure standing in a dark door-way.

Agnes's shoulders slumped.

Chapter Six

"As for the night she died, I only know up to about nine o'clock that night." Helen shifted, the couch cushion beneath her seemingly pulling her into the furniture itself. "Jolie had a wedding she was working."

Across from her, Agnes flashed a reassuring smile. "Did she attend the weddings she planned?"

"Oh, yes. She was committed. Beginning to end. That was her philosophy." The strange combination of wistful remembrance and painful sadness had her on edge. But with Malcolm sitting quietly for once, occupied with watching everything Heath was doing, and Veronica out of sight at the table behind her, she could focus on Agnes. For some reason, that made her calmer.

"Were you at the wedding with her?" Agnes asked.

"No. I was working late, actually. But we were texting." Helen rubbed her hands together, an old habit. She mimicked the act of scrubbing up before surgery. The familiar movements soothed her nerves. Malcolm always said it was a tell that she was nervous or had something weighing heavily on her mind.

"And your last text was at nine?"

"Around then, yes."

"So tell me, in your words, what you know of her activities that day."

Helen took a deep breath, rolled her shoulders, and let the breath out slowly. She opened her mouth to speak when Veronica's voice sounded through the room. "Remember, only what you actually know. No speculation."

"I met her for a quick lunch. It was a wedding day, so she didn't have much time, and I had surgeries, so neither did I. We met at this falafel food truck near the hospital. It was a frequent spot for us to catch a quick bite." Helen swallowed back her grief. She hadn't been back to that truck and had no intention of going back.

"What time was that?" Agnes asked. She slid her fingers through a hunk of shiny brown hair. Helen couldn't help but follow the curve of the hair as it shone in the light from the lamp beside her.

"Um...I think it was around one o'clock. The police kept pushing me for an exact time, but I just don't have it. I know I ended my last surgery at 12:43. But it takes awhile after that to get from surgery, ungown, and leave the building. I didn't look at a clock again. But I know I got back by 1:35, because that's when I checked on my patient."

"So it was short?"

"Yes. Jolie had already ordered and picked up the food when I met up with her at the truck. We sat on a little concrete ledge outside the bank building, ate, and talked."

"What did you talk about?" Agnes cocked her head. That cute little movement hit Helen in the gut every time.

"I don't remember all of the conversation. But I know we talked about the wedding she had that night. It was one of her discount weddings."

"Discount wedding? What does that mean?" Veronica asked.

Helen almost forgot her ex-cousin-in-law was hidden back there at the dining room table. She turned her head to see Veronica looking up from her tablet, one perfectly waxed eyebrow raised.

Helen turned back toward Agnes who grinned. "I'd like to know, too."

"Well, most of the weddings Jolie does...did...were high end. She charged a lot, and only the wealthy could afford her fees. But every once in a while, she did a pro bono gig. Well, it wasn't exactly pro bono. It was at cost. Usually she did them for LGBTQ weddings. But this was different. It was between a woman who just won her third battle with cancer and her high school sweetheart who she reconnected with during her chemo treatments. He was her nurse."

"Cool story," Heath said.

Agnes smiled again, her gaze fixed on Helen. "Yes. It is."

"Honestly," Helen said, "she could have afforded to do it for free. Stuff like that is why I wasn't sure if we'd be long-term or not." Helen ran a hand over her eyes. "I don't know. Maybe I shouldn't say things like that."

"Not important," Veronica said.

A soft hand landed on her knee, and Helen's head snapped up. "There's nothing wrong with telling the truth, even after someone passes." Agnes's voice was soft and comforting.

Helen swallowed back another lump. Agnes waited for a long beat before asking the next question. "So after that, you texted?"

What had been in Helen's head—and she was certain in everyone else's, too—was the phrase "that was the last time you saw her alive." But thankfully, Agnes hadn't said that. Helen took a deep breath. "Yes. We texted several more times that day. But...um...I deleted the texts. It was...I don't know. I was kind of melting down when it happened." Helen sat up straight. "But, um, I kind of remember what they were about."

"Wait. We aren't going to talk about fuzzy memories of texts that may or may not have happened," Veronica said.

Agnes was nonplussed about Veronica's attorney-like interruption. "No worries. I assume it was all mundane stuff. The usual?"

"Yes," Helen said. "Nothing worth remembering. I only remember the last text." Her chest quivered as she inhaled deeply. She tried to steady herself on the exhale. "She said she was leaving the reception soon, she was exhausted, and she'd call me tomorrow."

"And when did you hear about what happened?" Agnes's voice was as soft as the gentle squeeze she laid on Helen's knee. But the awkward position, leaned across the space between them, couldn't be sustained for long. Helen grieved the loss of the touch when Agnes leaned back.

"Not until the next afternoon. It was about an hour and a half before I met you, actually. Detective Poll caught me coming out of surgery. He told me Jolie died, no other explanation. He said he needed me to come to the station with him. I was completely confused. Totally lost. I got into his car. When we got to the station, he deposited me in the lobby and went in the back. I guess you know the rest." Helen shrugged.

Agnes's smile was bright. Helen hoped their first meeting was as memorable to Agnes as it was to her.

"So what happened in the interview room?"

"No way." The chair Veronica sat in scraped loudly against the hardwood floor as she shot out of her seat and ran around the couch to stand between Helen and Agnes. "We're not talking about a police interrogation that occurred when she didn't have an attorney present."

"Interrogation?" Agnes asked.

Veronica shook her head. "I meant interview."

"Did they accuse you?" Agnes asked.

Veronica whirled around to point her finger at Helen. "Not a word."

Helen sighed. She pushed Veronica's hand aside and craned her neck around to see Agnes, who nodded. "No problem."

Looking stunned, Veronica sank onto the couch beside Helen. "Okay. Good."

"So...do you have any other questions?" Helen asked.

"One more for today. Who do you think killed Jolie?"

The silence in the room pulsed with tension that matched the beating of Helen's heart. She'd had a person in mind since the moment Detective Poll broke the news. But she'd never said it out loud to anyone. She was scared of being wrong and terrified of being right. But it didn't matter, because Veronica wasn't having any of it.

"Whoa, whoa, whoa. We're not going to be doing any speculating here."

Agnes leaned forward. "That's not really what I—"

"No offense," Veronica said, "but this isn't my first rodeo. I know what the media does. And to be frank, I know what shows like *True Crime Tonight* do. You try to get everyone worked up, so they'll point fingers and sling accusations."

The need to defend Agnes rose like a rocket in Helen's

chest. She stood and moved to the center of the room. Her brain was formulating a great speech when Agnes beat her to it. "I understand completely why you would feel that way. I get it. Even though we try to be more on the up and up than other shows like ours, we can definitely come close to the line sometimes. But a few things are different about this story."

Veronica unfolded her arms and leaned forward. "I'm listening."

"For one, what we're working on here is a podcast, not a segment for the show. That might happen later, or it might not. Helen hasn't agreed to that yet. The podcast is the long game. We're trying to create a full and complete picture of Jolie's life and death by talking to a lot of different people. It's not the same as a snippet on one episode of television."

Veronica's lip twisted up. Her brows rose expectantly.

Agnes let out a long breath, sat up straight, and continued. "And secondly, it's personally important to me to get this story right. Jolie and I had a thing as teenagers. I'm queer and I want this story told right."

Veronica sat back in her seat. A huff of breath accompanied the action. "I see."

"Okay," Helen said. "I think we've harassed Agnes enough for one day. You want me to answer the question?"

Agnes spoke quickly. "No. Let's just end today's session here. Thank you, everyone."

A deep silence settled over the room as Heath packed up. Veronica and Malcolm lingered, which prevented Helen from having any potential alone time with Agnes. But as Agnes slipped past Helen on her way to the door, she slid her hand against Helen's wrist. The tiny touch, unnoticed by everyone else, sent an unfamiliar shockwave through Helen's body.

****

"Mr. Tamron. I'm so glad to have the opportunity to speak with you." Agnes practically jumped out of her skin when the man himself finally answered on the eighteenth

call. Heath leaned closer to the phone Agnes held in front of
her, propped on the paper-littered surface of her desk. The
two leather chairs they perched in barely fit in the space,
and Heath half-sat in Gretchen's area with his torso
stretched awkwardly toward the phone. Comfort be damned,
there was no way either member of this crime discovery
team was going to miss the chance to talk to Derek Green's
attorney. "I'm Agnes—"

"I know who you are." Thick and deep, his voice
matched the images they'd pulled up online of a man with a
round belly and a bushy white beard.

"Great. Then you know we're working on a podcast as
well as a story for the *True Crime Tonight* television show."

"What, exactly, is it you want. And be brief," he grumbled.

"I'd like to talk to your client and get his thoughts on
this tragic thing that happened to Jolie. Hear..." Agnes
stopped herself from saying "his side of story" to choose
more tempered language. "Hear what he has to say about her
life and death."

A long pause, peppered with harsh breaths from the
other end of the line, ended with Mr. Tamron saying, "You
can submit a list of questions to me."

"Does that mean he'll answer them in writing or consider an interview or—"

"Submit no more than six questions tomorrow and I'll
contact you." The statement was followed by a distinctive
click.

Agnes and Heath stared at one another, both with
dropped chins. "Does that mean we'll get something?"
Heath asked.

"I have no idea. But I'm sure as hell going to try." The
lights dimmed in the building as the last person besides
them left. Agnes turned on the bright lamp above her desk
and reached for the Chinese take-out menu. "Even if I have
to be here all night."

"Can I stay and help?" Heath asked.

She hadn't expected that. But Heath had been surprising
her a lot lately, and Agnes had to wonder if she'd been an
ass jumping to conclusions about him. "Sure. Pick what you

want." She handed him the slightly crumpled paper menu.

Deciding which of the forty tempting items on the menu they wanted to eat proved to be far easier than drafting six questions for the man whose ex-wife had been mysteriously murdered.

"We have to ask him about that night specifically," Heath said.

Agnes ran a hand over her chin. "I agree, but it's all about working up to it."

"I get it," Heath said. "I've seen you in action. Your ability to tease answers out of people is incredible. But this time we don't have the advantage of getting to talk them through it. My concern is that they'll answer the easy questions and leave the hard ones blank."

"Hell, they could leave them all blank. This 'put it in writing' thing is bullshit."

"Yeah. But it's all we have."

Agnes glanced at her partner. No matter how they began their collaboration, they were truly a team now, and Heath proved his worth every day. "Okay. So what should we start with?"

"Where were you on the night of the murder?"

"Won't he just repeat his alibi?"

Heath gestured in the air. "Let him. We haven't heard the alibi word for word. Let's hear it ourselves."

"Right." Each question was precious. Agnes hesitated to waste any words, but Heath was right. They were investigating in their own right. "Let's do it."

Heath's brows hit his hairline. "Yeah?"

"Yeah. What else?"

Heath rubbed his hands together. "We should find out why he was at the apartment so much when he was supposed to have moved out."

"Let's ask him to describe his relationship with Jolie at the time of her death, including how often they saw each other. It's less accusatory."

"Great. What else?"

Agnes poked at the underside of her chin with her pen while Heath typed the questions out. "We need to get to the heart of their marriage."

"And divorce."

"Yes. Let's leave it open-ended. Ask him to tell us in his own words about the marriage."

Heath's fingers flew across the keyboard. "Then another question about the divorce."

"Yep. And that leaves the big one."

Heath's head snapped up, and his gaze bored into Agnes. "Yeah? What's the big one?"

"We have to ask him what he thinks happened to Jolie."

A half-hour later, they had wordsmithed the questions to death and were breaking to eat yummy Chinese take-out from cardboard containers.

"You think this Derek guy is guilty as hell?" Heath asked.

Agnes chewed on her Egg Foo Young and tossed the chopsticks into the container on her lap. She stared into Heath's sky-blue eyes. "It's too soon to tell. We don't have shit so far."

Heath set his own carton of Orange Chicken on the desk beside Agnes's computer and used his fingers to tick off his points. "We know the nosey neighbor says he was there that night. We know they were newly divorced. He had his own place. She was changing the locks, presumably to keep him out. And the nosey neighbor says they fought all the time." Having used up his entire hand, he slapped it on his knee.

Agnes couldn't entirely suppress her amused grin. "I take it you think he's guilty?"

"Hell yeah, I do. I mean, just on statistics alone, it's most likely the spouse, right? But also, this guy is super sketchy."

Agnes held up her water bottle. "Well, it sounds like you solved it. I mean, forget the thirty-two people who saw him at the pub during the time of the murder." She took a drink and lowered the bottle to the desk with a dull thud. She picked up her carton to finish off her dinner. "We should call the cops and tell them."

Heath rolled his eyes at her sarcasm. "Whatever." He picked up his own carton from the desk and poked through it with a white, plastic fork. "What do you think of Helen?" he asked, eyes still on the contents of the cardboard box.

"What do you mean?"

Heath raised his head and met her gaze. "I like her. She's this quiet, honest, doctor. Great eyes. Killer legs."

Agnes slapped his chest playfully. "Are you being a pig?"

"No. I'm being honest. She rocked that skirt today."

Agnes rubbed a hand over her favorite black slacks. Helen had looked amazing in a blue pencil skirt that highlighted her well-toned legs. It seemed the three or four inches of height she had on Agnes were all carried in the lower part of her body.

Rather than continue along that train of thought, or conversation for that matter, Agnes went back to something else Heath had said. "How do you know she's honest?"

He shrugged and his big shoulders strained the tight, grey T-shirt he wore. "My mom always said I had good intuition about people. Like I can tell if they're an asshole or something. I've known a lot of assholes, and I've known a lot of good people. She's good people."

Agnes took a moment to try and picture what Heath's mother must be like. But she couldn't quite form the image. Heath was still a pile of contradictions that made her own intuition about him fuzzy.

"You didn't answer my question," Heath said. "What do you think of Helen?"

What Agnes thought was that Helen was beautiful, smart, and intriguing. She was attracted to her in a way she hadn't been to a woman in a very long time. But she wasn't going to reveal any of that to Heath, or anyone else. This was her job, her livelihood. Professionalism beat out emotions. It had to.

"We'll see," she said.

****

A strange vibe filled the hospital's surgical wing, or at least the ten-foot bubble around Helen as she moved through it.

People she'd worked with for two years mumbled hellos, while hustling by, when they used to stop to talk. Others saw her coming down a narrow hallway and turned to go the opposite way.

She breezed into the scrub room, working hard to keep her head up and her confidence from plunging through the floor. She had a surgery to do, a life to save. "Hi, Wendy," she said. "How was your weekend?"

Dr. Wendy Milford was just finishing up. She was headed toward surgery room six, which was attached through a set of swinging doors opposite the ones Helen would soon go through to access surgical room five. Wendy swung her head around like she'd been startled. Hands up, frozen on the spot, she stared blankly at Helen.

Helen's smile faltered as Wendy's eyes bored through her. "Helen," she finally said. Helen waited for more words, but none came. Instead Wendy turned on her heel, disappeared through the swinging doors, and left that single word hanging in the air.

Helen shook her head as if to shake off the interaction. She pushed everything to the back of her mind for the next four hours: Jolie's absence in her life, her mysterious death, the hours she'd spent in a police interview room, Veronica's intensity, Malcolm's protectiveness, and Agnes's kind eyes. She focused on Mr. Jansen. Careful, methodical work was going to keep Mr. Jansen alive for many more years to enjoy his twenty-two grandchildren.

After the surgery, Helen spoke to Mr. Jansen's sweet and gracious wife, tense and nervous daughters, and a few of the older grandchildren before walking into the office area to finish charting and check on her schedule for the next day.

Her favorite person at the hospital was there, James Hobart. Despite being chief of cardiovascular surgery, he was a soft-spoken, laid-back man who was always ready with an easy laugh, a dad joke, or a shoulder to cry on. If she could count her boss among her friends, she would.

James pulled her into a hug as soon as she crossed the threshold to the room. Then he pushed her back to arm's length to examine her closely. "How are you doing? You look like hell."

"Gee, thanks."

"I mean it. Are you sleeping?"

Helen moved out of his grasp and plunked down in a chair at the table that held her charts, placed there by one of the nurses. She sat sideways so she could still face James while resting her weary bones. "A little." She ran a hand over her face. "I'll be okay."

"Wanna come over for dinner this week?" He pulled another chair from the desk opposite her and sat down in front of her, their knees nearly touching. He leaned forward and deep worry lines traveled across his brow. "Tilly would love to see you. We'll make veggie burgers."

She loved that he was so willing to accommodate her chosen diet. "Sounds good."

"Great. Saturday night, then."

She nodded as he rose. "I have two surgeries tomorrow, right? I'll need a break by the end of this week if I keep going like this."

James turned, his expression unreadable. "About that."

Helen cocked her head and squinted her eyes. "Yes?"

"Mike Miller cancelled."

"Cancelled? He needs a bypass. You can't just cancel a bypass." She was alarmed. Mike Miller's case was pretty dire.

"He's going to do the surgery. Just not with you. I offered to do it."

It took Helen a long moment to climb out of the confusion muddling her brain. "I don't understand."

James sat back down, leaned forward, and took one of Helen's hands in his own. "He didn't want you to do it. Because of the news."

"About me being a person of interest in Jolie's case?"

James nodded.

"About me being in a lesbian relationship?"

James shrugged, but doubt was spelled across his features.

"Is that why everyone's treating me like a pariah all of a sudden?"

James squeezed her hand. "This is a welcoming hospital. No one should be judging another person based on their gender or sexual orientation—"

She held up her hand. "Save the lecture on inclusiveness, James. Even if that's not an issue, they all think I'm a killer, right?"

"Of course not. We're behind you. We're with you." He patted her shoulder. "You let me know if anyone gives you a hard time. But, honestly, we're a family. I expect the staff to support you, just like I do."

Helen managed to give James a weak smile and reassure him that she was probably just imagining things when she thought the staff were being stand-offish. Once he was gone, and she was alone, Helen pulled her phone out of the side pocket of her white lab coat. She didn't hesitate as she probably should have. Instead, she immediately hit the contact for Agnes and waited as the phone rang.

"Helen, hi." Agnes's voice was bright and cheery.

Helen let out a breath. Her shoulders fell for the first time all day. She leaned back in her chair. "Hi."

"How are you?" Agnes asked.

Helen's voice broke as the wave of pressures bore down on her. "Not great."

"Is everything okay? What am I saying? Of course it isn't. Where are you?"

"I'm at the hospital."

"You know that little ice cream shop across the street from the ER entrance?"

"Yes."

"Meet me there in ten, if you can."

"I'll be there." Helen felt a light in her future for the first time in days. That light was Agnes.

Chapter Seven

Helen moved through the door of the shop like she was dragging a dead body behind her. The slumped shoulders, deep frown, and sad eyes did nothing to dampen her beauty though. Her blue wrap-around dress, hitting just above the knee, and her heels showed off her killer legs—as Heath had called them—and her soft hair floated around her head like a cloud over sunshine, even if that sunshine was slightly eclipsed by a dark mood.

Agnes didn't need to wave to get Helen's attention. The doctor honed right in on her sitting at a booth near the cash register. A little light came back into Helen's face, and Agnes hoped it was because of her.

"I'm so happy to see you." Helen slumped into the booth opposite Agnes. Nearly as soon as she said it, her eyes grew wide and her mouth parted as if she couldn't believe she'd just said what she did.

"Long day?" Agnes asked.

"They all seem to be long lately. A binge on a hot fudge sundae is exactly what I need."

Agnes passed the single-page, paper menu over to Helen. "I'm getting the Death by Chocolate."

Helen took the menu but didn't look at it. "That's exactly what I need! Done."

Agnes felt Helen's desperation and made eye contact with the waitress who'd given her water and a menu a few minutes before. The woman was competent and quick. It took only a moment to put in their orders.

With chocolate comfort on the way, Agnes turned back to Helen. "Wanna talk about it?"

Helen sighed. "Maybe not yet."

"Fine. Then I'll tell you about my day," Agnes said.

Helen rested her elbow on the laminate tabletop and

propped her chin in the heel of her hand. "I'd like that."

"It started with my coffeemaker exploding. Apparently it's been in desperate need of a cleaning for a while, and I've been ignoring it. The thing is, I live on coffee. It was essential I find a way to get it, preferably without slurping it up off the counter with my tongue. So I rushed through my shower and got dressed. Don't you hate a fast shower?"

"I always shower at night," Helen said.

"Oh. I guess that makes sense. Wash the hospital off."

"Get the knots of tension out of my neck, too."

Helen relaxed, so Agnes decided to keep talking. "I popped into the coffee shop a block from the BART. The train was packed, so I had to stare at the stupid cup of coffee the whole ride because I get weirded out drinking when people are so close to me. I'm afraid they'll breathe on my coffee if I remove the little cover stick they put in the hole of the lid. It's weird. Anyway, when I got off—I shit you not—I ducked into an alley to guzzle half my twenty-ouncer like a drug addict hiding their hit. Then I ran to the office and was five minutes late to the morning meeting. We have a meeting every damn morning. Do you have to do that?"

"No," Helen said as a small, amused smile painted her lips. "We have meetings, but not everyday, thank God, unless you count meeting with other doctors about a patient. We do that. But it's different doctors every time, and it's less like a meeting and more like...caring for someone. I don't know."

"I think it's so cool what you do," Agnes said.

Helen shrugged and gazed down at the table. The shy, demure look was too adorable. "Malcolm and I think what you do is pretty fascinating."

"Sometimes it is. It can be pretty emotionally draining as well. Murder takes its toll."

Helen frowned. "It's been so hard to wrap my head around the reality of someone I know, someone I care about, being murdered. It's surreal on top of being agonizing and horrible and...I don't even know what else. There's so much."

"There is," Agnes agreed. "I've watched other people

go through it. I could always sympathize, you know. In some cases, their pain was so tangible I felt it. I cried. I had trouble sleeping. I thought I understood it. But now it's different. It's closer to me." Agnes gazed into Helen's eyes. A string of understanding and compassion seemed to run between them, tying them together over that little table at the ice cream shop.

The string was abruptly severed by a pair of hands delivering two massive glass dishes piled high with ice cream, chocolate, nuts, and whipped cream. Identical bright, red cherries perched precariously on top of each.

They thanked the waitress and assured her they didn't need anything else. Then, in a shared silence, they ate. Ravenous with grief and a very bad day, they gazed at each other over the sundaes as they moved gooey goodness from the dishes into their mouths. Bright brown eyes met murky hazel ones, locked in a long gaze that shut out everything else.

"You ready to talk about your bad day?" Agnes asked. Her focus finally left Helen as she scraped the bottom of her dish with the long, slender spoon, attempting to pick up the last liquid remains of her sundae.

The clink of metal on glass signaled Helen's spoon settling with finality into her own dish. "Yes. God that was good."

Agnes gazed up at the beautiful woman across from her. Helen leaned back in the booth bench. "People are looking at me like I'm...you know." She cocked her head, eyes damp.

Agnes knew Helen didn't want to say the word "guilty." So she nodded. "Yeah. So that's been happening?"

Helen swallowed back her tears as she nodded. "And today I found out one of my patients rescheduled his surgery with a different surgeon, my boss actually, my friend. I know it's just...I know this man doesn't know me that well. He's a patient, not a close friend. I know I'm not supposed to take things like that personally. Patients get second opinions. They switch doctors for any old reason. Especially when the doctor is young and just starting out. But him switching because of this...it feels like a betrayal. It feels like...people think...they think I'm..."

Agnes's heart ached as Helen buried her head in her hands. She reached out and placed a hand on Helen's elbow. Helen lifted her head. As their eyes met, she slipped her arm down and placed her hand in Agnes's waiting one.

"It's all going to work out," Agnes said softly, hoping like hell that was true. The quiet, unassuming doctor deserved much better.

Using her free hand, Helen wiped at her eyes. "I'm sorry I'm unloading all this on you."

Agnes squeezed Helen's slender fingers. "I'm pretty sure I asked you to."

Helen responded with a weak smile. "Why?"

The question was loaded. Maybe Helen was asking if Agnes was using Helen's distress to further her story. The answer to that was an unequivocal no. But before she made the assumption that such a cynical view had been adopted by a woman like Helen, she thought maybe Helen simply wanted to know where Agnes's interest in her lie. There was no easy answer to that. So she chose to change directions altogether and tell the honest-to-God truth. "You and me. We get each other."

****

Sweat beaded on Helen's forehead. Her eyes were sticky and fought opening. Her brain was still filled with the images from her dream. She clutched her head and tried to ground herself. Her lungs emitted heavy, panting breaths.

The image the dream ended on hovered above her still-closed eyes: Agnes lying beneath her, eyes half-closed, neck strained as her head reached back, mouth open on a cry of ecstasy.

Jolie used to ask Helen, during their flirty texts, if she dreamed about her. It had been the result of her admitting once that she was prone to sex dreams. She always said yes, even if it wasn't true.

Now that proclivity was coming back to bite her. Sexy dreams about Agnes were not what she needed right now. It only further clouded the "Agnes issue" that was growing more complicated by the day.

Yes, she was growing to trust Agnes, even though she wasn't sure she should. Veronica warned her daily to tread lightly where Agnes was concerned. She'd throw a fit if she knew Helen had met up with Agnes alone last night.

She was deeply attracted to Agnes, had been since she'd first seen her in the police station lobby. The timing for any attraction was terrible right now, but she couldn't deny that base emotion grew stronger each day.

Her feelings for Agnes were becoming more complex each time they spoke. Tingles ran up her spine when they had stared into each other's eyes over ice cream. And prickles of intense desire hit her when they touched.

Helen pulled herself into a sitting position, shoved a pillow behind her back, and reached for her phone on the nightstand. She needed advice, and she needed it now. Fortunately, her favorite shoulder was an early riser.

"Hi, punkin." The sound of Malcolm's heavy breath indicated he was on his morning run. "You have an early surgery?"

Helen had been known to call him on her way to work. If she had to be there early, he was on his run, later he was usually driving to see about a dog. Tears welled up in her eyes. "No. They gave me a few days off."

A long pause followed. Helen suspected Malcolm understood the significance of her statement. A surgeon being given a few days off usually meant a mistake had been made or a medical review was happening. It was never good. "What happened?" he finally asked.

"Nothing in particular," she said, repeating James's words when he called late the night before to tell her the hospital wanted her to take some administrative leave. "They just think I'm too stressed out. James is going to handle my patient load."

Malcolm's heavy breaths filled the air for a few long moments. Helen knew he was deciding whether or not to probe her vague reply further. In the end, he gave her a break. "So why are you up so early? You should be sleeping in."

"I need your advice on something."

Malcolm laughed, the sound rich and light in her ears. "There are only two things you ever ask me advice on."

Helen scratched her temple. "There are?"

"Yes," he said, as a true authority on the subject.

"Um. What are those two things?"

There was another chuckle. "Either you have some furniture to put together, or you want advice on women."

Helen couldn't repress her grin. "You got me."

"It's a little early for furniture building, so I'm guessing you had a sex dream?"

"Oh my God. Why do I tell my lovers about that?"

Malcolm laughed. "Since you sometimes talk in your sleep, it's not really a choice."

"I had a dream about Agnes," she admitted.

"Can't blame you there. She's smokin' hot."

Helen grinned. She and Malcolm had always been good at talking about women. They were so good at friendship, it's a wonder they ever thought they could be more. "Yes. She is. And she's doing a story on me."

"So?"

"So...I shouldn't be dreaming about her."

"By the way she looks at you, I'm guessing she wouldn't mind."

Malcolm threw the statement out there casually, but Helen greeted it with a jolt. Agnes had been kind, understanding, and incredibly approachable. But it hadn't occurred to Helen for a minute that Agnes might be attracted to her.

Her scientist instincts kicked in immediately. "What are you basing this on?"

"My ability to read people."

Helen released a distinctive scoff right into the phone, so there was no mistaking she doubted his abilities. But it was a lie. She'd always trusted Malcolm's opinions on people, even though she'd never let him know that. A definite balance was required to keep his ego in check.

"I'm going to need more than that," she said.

"Look. I know when someone wants you. Man or

woman. I know it when I see it. And I'm telling you, that woman wants some Helen magic."

A nervous laugh escaped her. "I don't know what to say."

"Don't say anything to me. Say something to her."

Helen let out a long, slow breath then sucked it back in, one molecule at a time. She trusted Malcolm's impressions of people. He could have been a shrink if he hadn't gone into dog training. So his answer to her next question was far more weighted than she wanted to admit. "So, um, should I trust her?"

"You know, I'd rather throw myself in front of a bus than be wrong about that and have you get hurt," he said. "So, I'm not going to give you a yes or no just yet."

"But it's not a no?"

"It's definitely not a no."

Chapter Eight

"You actually got a response from Derek's attorney?" Malcolm looked as shocked as Agnes felt.

"He's not stupid." Veronica was the only one who seemed to be confident this would happen. "He knows he can't blow off the media entirely. It makes him look guilty. So he gives just enough to be able to say he cooperated but not enough to give you anything." She looked down at her perfectly manicured, baby-blue nails. "I bet the answers were about as useful as the ones you get at a presidential debate. Am I right?"

Agnes chuckled. There was something unfathomably likable about Veronica. "Pretty much. He claims he was there that evening, as the neighbor said, but that he was only gathering up some of his things. He said when Jolie came home, they talked briefly, then he left. He said she was alive and well when he walked out the door."

"But there are no witnesses to that," Heath interjected. "And the neighbor lady was sure that whoever she did see leave that night wasn't Derek."

"Please tell me the apartment complex has a camera," Malcolm said.

Agnes liked this camaraderie in the search for a killer. It felt like a television show. But she also knew it went against all her training. She should be asking all the questions, giving out none of the information. And her tech guy definitely shouldn't be helping to spill all their beans. But she couldn't seem to help herself either. Something about this gave her a rush she never experienced before on a story.

"The apartment has lots of cameras," Agnes said. "But the power had been cut to every single one that was relevant to the case."

"Wait a minute." Malcolm sat forward on the couch,

jolting Helen's body beside him. "Someone cut the feed to only specific cameras?"

Agnes knew Heath was super into this detail. He'd made all the calls then gone to meet with the apartment manager to look at the cut wires in the box. Agnes had handed the assignment over to him after seeing his infectious enthusiasm. So when she turned her head to look at him, he jumped right in.

"Yeah, so there's a box outside the office. The wires for the cameras are centralized there. It's pretty old-school tech. Anyway, someone cut the wires to the front door, the elevator entrance in the lobby, and the elevator exit and hallway view on Jolie's floor. The rest were left intact."

"Inside job," Malcolm said.

Heath nodded enthusiastically.

"Inside where?" Veronica asked. "I mean, someone who works at the apartment complex, a contractor, the security company, the power company?"

Heath's forehead scrunched up. "Good question."

Silence blanketed the room as wheels turned in their heads. Agnes watched with a combination of fascination and humor. Finally, Heath slumped back in his chair. "I'll figure it out."

"So, what do you know about Derek?" Agnes asked Helen.

Helen had been sitting quietly during this conversation about what Derek's attorney had given them in response to their questions, which had been—as Veronica predicted—a whole lot of nothing. Her big brown eyes gazed at Agnes. "Not much. I know the marriage was bad. Jolie tried for a long time to get a divorce. He fought it. They had money, and he used it to get an attorney who blocked her at every turn and dragged the whole thing out."

"Who did the money belong to?"

"Jolie did well in her business, but Derek has family money. The thing is, his parents don't like him much. They put his trust fund in Jolie's name when they got married so he wouldn't blow it all, or so Jolie said. She gave the trust back to his parents in the divorce, rather than to him. I'm sure it's weird for a thirty-year-old man to have his wife and parents dole out his allowance." Helen shrugged, her sad eyes still fixed on Agnes. "It all sounded strange to me, but also contentious, you know?" She glanced over at Malcolm, and the pair shared a smile.

It was clear as day to Agnes that Helen and Malcolm didn't have a difficult divorce. They exposed the dream breakup with every tender glance.

"So Derek hated that they got divorced. What else?"

"He definitely didn't like that he lost access to his money."

"Was he violent with her?"

Helen's lips turned down. "I hope not. But I don't know. We didn't talk about him much. She said he was her past. She wanted to get over and away from him."

Helen's gentleness was apparent in every move she made. It was cute, endearing, and a bit of a turn-off. Which was probably a good thing, because Agnes spent entirely too much time thinking about Helen's big, brown eyes, soft skin, and incredible legs. Assuming that Helen wasn't her type in bed might help her focus.

"What about their living situation? Did he still stay there?"

Helen shook her head vehemently. "No. And she didn't want him there. She was trying to get the locks changed, but there was a delay. That's probably why he was there that night. I doubt she was happy about it."

"I doubt that as well." Agnes glanced at the responses from Derek's attorney, screaming back at her from the lit tablet in her lap. She said, "He admits he was there that night, and that she didn't want him there. He wanted her to give him money, and she wouldn't. There's a lot of math there that adds up to suspicion on Derek."

"I looked into this." Veronica clicked her long, manicured nails. "She still had life insurance policies with Derek as the beneficiary. She hadn't changed them yet. I always tell my girls, first time the D word is mentioned, change those life insurance policies."

Heath whistled.

"That's pretty damning," Malcolm said.

"But the police aren't calling Derek a suspect," Helen said. "They haven't arrested him. They must know something we don't."

Heath leaned forward. "We know he has an alibi at the time of death. Thirty-two people saw him at a bar three blocks away when the medical examiner says Jolie died."

This was always the rub. The case against Derek seemed so obvious. But then there was his solid alibi. Thirty-two were a hell of a lot of witnesses, almost suspiciously so. But it was also way too many people to fool or manipulate. "Which brings us back to the mysterious third person."

Veronica stood up from her chair at the table behind Helen. "Please tell me you asked the attorney about the third person."

Agnes suppressed the "Of course" she wanted to say. "We did. He said Derek had no knowledge of any other person in the apartment, and if there was another person, they were there after he left."

"Except then there wouldn't be three," Heath said. "Math."

"Yeah. Math. Anyway, that's all we got on that." Agnes hit the button on the tablet to make the screen go dark, just like their theory of Derek as the killer.

Helen let out a long sigh. Agnes could tell this conversation was wearing on her. "Is there anything else you want to talk about?" Agnes asked.

Helen looked at the recording equipment in front of Heath and shook her head. Agnes nodded to Heath, who shut off the recording. She smiled at Helen and opened her mouth to thank her for another interview when Helen sat straighter and cleared her throat.

"Can I ask you a question?"

Agnes leaned toward her. "Anything."

"I wanna know..." She glanced around the room. All four people stared at her, stuck on her every word. Then she looked back to Agnes. "Are you looking for the truth here, or just a good story?"

Without hesitation, and with the knowledge that there was no lie in her words, Agnes said, "The truth. I promise."

****

The colors of the image on the television blurred together in Helen's eyes as her mind tried to keep up. Derek Green's face, broad and a bit too chiseled, took up most of the screen. His mouth moved with vicious slowness.

"All I want is justice for Jolie," he told the unseen reporter. "She was an amazing woman. She didn't deserve to be murdered like this."

Helen flinched, and her mind flashed to the words Detective Poll used during their first meeting. *Strangled to death slowly.* She and Derek might only agree on one thing—Jolie didn't deserve that; no one did.

"Do you have any idea who would do this?" the reporter asked Derek.

Helen shook her head to clear it of her morose thoughts. She tried to focus on Derek's words. His lips twisted into a sneer. "I've got an idea, all right." His head pivoted to the left as if he were consulting with someone. Then he turned back to the camera. "But my attorney says I need to keep that information between me and the police right now."

Surprisingly, the interviewer didn't push the issue; instead, he asked. "What can you tell us about the people in Jolie's life at the time of her death?"

The question seemed odd, out of place somehow. Helen was no reporter, but something about it just didn't sit right. Neither did Derek's answer.

"The most important person was probably her girlfriend." He stopped at that and let the emphasized word hang in the air.

"Yes. The surgeon, right? What can you tell us about her?"

"Dr. Helen Nims is interesting, all right," Derek said.

Helen's stomach rolled as she waited for what was to come. Her breath hitched, stuck in her throat, along with a cry of despair. Kimber cuddled closer to her, that mysterious dog instinct to comfort their distressed humans pulling her in.

How did she get here?

"My wife," Derek said, "was a naturally curious person. So when we were having trouble in our marriage, she was ripe for someone like the doctor to take advantage of her."

Helen nearly threw up. Right there on television, this man she'd never even met was completely changing the narrative and defaming her.

Derek scratched at the tawny hair cut short above his ears. "Jolie was so...gullible."

"Do you think Dr. Nims had something to do with your wife's murder?"

Stormy blue eyes pierced the lens of the camera, reaching through the glass screen of the television to stab Helen in the heart. "I'm not at liberty to say. I'll let you put two and two together."

The interviewer signed off, and the camera returned to the anchor desk. A story about a dog that played the piano started, and Helen slammed her head back against the couch. Her mind moved so quickly she couldn't discern one thought from another.

She was only weakly conscious of Kimber barking at the trick dog on the TV. Somehow, the ringing of the phone broke through the noise, jolting her away from her thoughts by the third set of tones. She sat up and managed to hush Kimber. Malcolm was calling over and over. She picked it up to make the birdsong ringtone that was uniquely his stop. "I can't talk right now."

"Helen, you have to talk to me." His voice echoed with desperation.

How did she tell her best friend in the world that he wasn't the person she wanted to confide in at that moment? "I will, I promise. But I think I should call Veronica first, don't you?"

Malcolm paused, his heavy breaths the indicator she needed to know he was calming himself down. "I guess."

"Where's that lovely lady you've been dating?"

"Um. She's here."

"Good. Go hang out with her and chill. I promise I'll call you later, okay?" The soothing tone of her voice seemed to come out of nowhere, but she was grateful for it.

"You sure?"

"Positive. I'm okay, Malcolm, I swear."

"Did you see the news?" A note of confusion colored his tone.

From a strength she didn't realize she had, Helen pulled out a laugh. "I did. That man is such a freaking joke. I'm not worried. But I do want to talk to Veronica. I'm sure I'll get some phone calls from the press, and I need to know what she wants me to say."

She heard the surprise in his voice as he agreed that was best and told her to remember to call him later. By the time she got him off the phone, she nearly fell apart. But she managed to make one more phone call before breaking down in tears.

Twenty minutes later, Agnes stood outside her apartment. Helen wiped up as much of the mess on her face as possible before throwing open the door. Agnes took one look at her and opened her arms. Helen fell into them.

Right there on the threshold to her house, Helen got her first full embrace from Agnes. Head to toe, they were connected. The sensation was both intensely comforting and incredibly sensual.

Through her grief and fear, the images of her dream about Agnes pushed their way into the melee in Helen's mind. Now those images were matched with the feel of Agnes's curvy body melding into Helen's sharper one in all the right places.

"Come on," Agnes said gently, pushing Helen through the entrance and closing the door behind her with one hand, while keeping the other around Helen's waist. She ushered Helen through the living room and settled them both, hip-to-hip, on the couch. Her arm stayed around Helen's waist, her hand providing a soothing pressure. "I'm here."

Having her core surrounded by Agnes moved Helen between comfort and excitement like a ping-pong ball bouncing around her busy mind, thrown haphazardly by her uncaring body. Helen turned her head and brought her face flush with Agnes. Eyes locked and breaths collided in the few inches between them. "Thank you for coming."

Agnes nodded slowly. Her head barely moved. "I'm here for you."

"I need to call Veronica to find out what to do."

Agnes nodded.

"But first I wanted...I wanted you," Helen said.

Agnes didn't say anything in response. Her eyes shifted in tiny movements as her gaze roamed Helen's face, racing from her eyes to her lips and back again. The air between them was thinner than that in the rest of the room. It was like a vacuum, a space that required closing.

Helen wasn't sure which of them moved first. It may have been one of those completely in-sync movements. Like swimmers leaving the blocks at the starting buzzer, they sprung into action at the exact same moment.

What was certain was the way their mouths crashed together created waves of desire surging through Helen. Before she was conscious of it, her tongue darted out to meet Agnes's, and their lips danced in a perfect ballet of need and want.

Helen pushed up on her knees, towering over Agnes, who let Helen push her back onto the couch. Once Agnes was exactly where Helen wanted her, lying beneath her, eyes wide, breath ragged, Helen pulled back and gazed down at the beauty. "You're gorgeous," she said, every bit of confidence a good kiss always brought out in her on display.

Agnes's face expressed a mixture of desire—pink lips parted, cheeks flushed, neck muscles strained—and shock— eyes wide, brows raised. The reaction was so foreign to Helen she had to ask, "Are you okay?"

Agnes stayed still for a long moment. Alarmed, Helen shifted back, butt landing on her heels. Had she just kissed someone who didn't want her? Had she been wrong about the magnetic field pulling them together?

Agnes sat up slowly, which brought her face back to the place it had been before they kissed, right in front of Helen. "I'm just...floored."

"Is that good or bad?" Helen was not at all sure what she was supposed to take from that one, cryptic word.

"Good...too good," Agnes said.

Helen couldn't stop her brow from scrunching up or her lips turning down in a frown. She was so confused. Agnes didn't clarify. She got up quickly and headed straight for the door, grabbing her purse in a single scoop as she passed it.

Before Helen could even find her breath again, Agnes was gone.

Chapter Nine

Agnes had sat with lots of families with ripped-out hearts. It was the hardest part of her job, looking into the faces of people so deeply cut by the loss of a loved one, their lives torn apart suddenly and violently.

Sitting with Jolie's mom and sister, however, made the other interviews look like a cakewalk. Still fresh from Helen's grief and need the night before and still processing her own wounds, Agnes was now confronted with grief so tangible it filled the room.

"She was so beautiful." Rita Hill swiped at her nose with a tissue. "You remember her from high school. Remember how beautiful she was?"

Agnes swallowed back her tears. "I do."

"Well she only got more beautiful. All my kids are gorgeous." Rita turned to look at one of her two surviving daughters, Kelly.

Kelly gazed back at her mom. "She was the prettiest of us all."

"I remember she was a good dancer, too," Agnes said.

"Yes," Rita said. "She took ballet from the time she was three years old. By the time she was twelve, she was doing solos at the recitals. She was so graceful."

"How did she get into wedding planning?" Agnes hoped to ease slowly toward the place they needed to eventually go.

Rita launched into a story about Jolie's experiences as a bridesmaid that coincided with her burgeoning career in event planning to land squarely on the perfect career for her. She and Kelly talked about how good Jolie was at her job and how she built a successful business from it.

They spent a little more time on general talk about Jolie. It was Rita who brought up Jolie's sexuality, much to

Agnes's relief. Heath sat beside her, quiet and still, nearly invisible through the whole thing.

"I never minded that she sometimes had girlfriends," Rita said. "Her dad was okay with it, too. He just wanted her to be happy. She even brought a nice girl to his funeral. Anyway, that wasn't a problem in our family."

Kelly said, "Our one brother wasn't a fan. But the rest of us gave him such a hard time about being an ass, he hasn't said a word about it in years."

"Can you tell me about her marriage to Derek?" Agnes finally asked.

The mood in the room turned dark and foreboding with the mere mention of his name. Agnes felt the tension rise. She saw that Heath's eyes were wide and his back straight as an arrow. She wasn't alone in sensing they were headed into dangerous territory.

"Edward had just passed when she started dating him," Rita said. "I figured it was some grief thing. None of us liked him. He was rich and smug and lazy."

Kelly nodded.

The fact that they were in a nice house not far from Agnes's parents' home—and Agnes knew exactly how much they'd paid for that home—didn't seem to change the narrative of these women at all, meaning that their idea of rich was really, really rich.

"How long did they date before they got married?"

"It was less than two months," Kelly said. "We thought it would end soon. Then the next thing we knew, she came back from Vegas married to him. Turns out it was his parents' idea. They were completely thrilled to have her take over responsibility for their loser son."

"It was practically a shotgun wedding—in reverse," Rita said.

Agnes took a moment to choose her next question. As she scrambled for the words, her eyes traced the pattern of the colorful flowers on the chair Rita perched on. "And the marriage. How was the marriage?"

"Awful," Rita said.

"Abusive," Kelly said.

"Abusive?" Agnes remembered Helen's quiet plea that she hoped that wasn't true. But here it was coming from Jolie's sister. "Are we talking emotionally or physically?"

"Both," Kelly said. "I saw bruises. She made excuses. But we knew the truth."

"So he was physically abusive?"

"Yes." Kelly left no room for doubt.

Agnes trained her gaze on Rita, who nodded sadly. "Her father would have pummeled that man."

Certainly a man could be an emotional abuser and kill his wife, and certainly a man could be a physical abuser and not kill his wife, but if there was one thing she'd learned in the true crime world it was that when a woman was dead and she had an abusive husband, red flags waved frantically.

"So...Jolie never admitted this to you?" Agnes was having a hard time reconciling the woman she'd known with a battered wife. But then, in a nanosecond, that changed. She knew better than that. Anyone could be a victim of domestic violence. Hadn't she seen that with her own eyes time and again?

"No. She always had some excuse for the injuries," Kelly said.

"And the divorce. What can you tell me about that?" Agnes asked.

"She finally stood up to him," Kelly said. "She was so fierce. So determined to get away. Our brother said she'd turned hard and mean, but I knew it was just part of the strength she had to have to get out of a bad situation. She was doing it, too. Until he killed her."

Heath and Agnes exchanged a look. The recorder was on. They'd just gotten gold, and they both knew it. "So, you think Derek killed Jolie?" Agnes asked.

"Yes," Rita said. "We absolutely do. We told the detectives as much."

Kelly rolled her eyes. "I can't believe they haven't arrested him. They're using his alibi and the 'third person' to drag their feet."

"Last night, Derek seemed to imply that Helen Nims had something to do with Jolie's death. What can you say about that?" Heath had asked that question. They'd agreed he would. Agnes couldn't bring herself to even talk about what that vile creature had said about Helen.

"Bullshit," Kelly said. "We met Helen. We all did. Jolie brought her over to dinner not long after they started dating. Which was after the divorce, by the way. She was lovely. Everyone liked her, even my asshole brother."

"He's just picking on that sweet doctor lady because he's jealous," Rita said.

"Jealous and guilty," Kelly added.

Agnes let out a breath. At least these women were two less people who considered Helen a viable suspect. "What else can you tell us about Derek?"

"His family is loaded," Kelly said. "Derek's father started a successful electronics company back in the eighties, and it boomed."

"His parents seemed nice enough." Rita placed her hand on her heart. "I met them after the wedding. They couldn't stop telling me how glad they were that Jolie married Derek. They were a hell of a lot happier than I was, I'll tell you that."

"Yeah, Jolie got the runt of the litter," Kelly said.

"What do you mean by that?" Agnes was fascinated by the expression.

Rita shook her head. "There are five kids. All of them are involved in the business. All of them are hard-working and respectable, except for Derek. He just lazed around and lived off his family's money."

"He's the oldest, but it's his younger brother that's the star of the family," Kelly said.

"Younger?"

Kelly nodded. "Only other boy and youngest in the family. Just as good-looking as Derek, but twice the man. He's being groomed to be the company's next CEO. I don't know why the hell Jolie didn't marry him."

Rita nodded. "Erik is a very nice man. And single." She switched directions and shook her head again. "He would have made a good husband. But, no, my baby had to marry the bad one."

Agnes was certain these two women were calling the detectives daily to harass them about arresting Jolie's murderer. "What do the police tell you about Derek?"

"Ugh," Kelly said with a groan. "Don't get me started."

But that was exactly what Agnes wanted to do. "Are they giving you the runaround?"

"Yes and no," Kelly said. "Detective Poll is very considerate. He calls regularly to give us updates on the case."

"Updates with no information," Rita said.

Agnes was all too familiar with that tactic. "Have you discussed Derek with him?"

"You bet we have," Kelly said. "We brought him up day one, and we bring him up every time we talk to anyone at SFPD."

Rita scowled. "They always say the same thing. He has a rock-solid alibi."

Agnes wished she could tell them she'd found a way around that alibi. But she hadn't. And what did that mean for Helen?

****

The crowded restaurant proved to be unexpected cover for Helen. For the first time since Derek's television interview, she didn't feel like a fish in a bowl in public. The people were enjoying themselves and their well-made food without paying a lick of attention to her.

"How are you, Helen. I've been worried about you," James said.

"I've been worried about whether or not I still have a job." James was one of a handful of people she could be so blunt with.

"You have a job. Of course you do." James leaned his elbows on the table. "This administrative leave is temporary. We'd like to bring you back in a week or two. We just want to make sure you're in a good place. I want to make sure you're in a good place. And I want to know what I can do to help."

Helen let out her breath. She trusted James. But she didn't trust anyone above him. She didn't fully believe that her job wasn't in jeopardy. "My attorney says you have to give an explanation for the leave."

"Yes. I reminded the hospital counsel. Since you're getting paid, they have a certain amount of time, and... Look, I'm not here to be hospital administration. I'm here as your friend."

Helen made her best attempt at a smile. She understood that James wanted to keep this social. But her few days of leave had turned into almost two weeks. She needed answers. Instead of pushing, though, she talked to her friend. "I'm doing okay. Malcolm has been great."

"He's a good guy."

"Yes. He is. And I'm doing this podcast thing. I don't know if it's a good idea. But it feels kind of cathartic." She lifted up her wineglass. "So does this."

James laughed, the little crinkle lines around his eyes forming a familiar sight. Helen almost relaxed. But something was off. Their server brought their dinners in what had to be record time. Helen felt the woman's eyes boring into her as she set the plates on the table and lingered to ask what else they needed. Instead of dealing with that, she looked around the room.

This little hideaway had become more and more popular in the last few years, as word got out about the great food and generous drink pours. It was within walking distance from a BART station and had great atmosphere. It was only a matter of time until each table was full and there was standing room only in the small lobby.

She and James had a reservation, which meant they were sitting in a prime spot in a booth along the wall. It gave her a full view of the tables in the center of the room and most of the booths. Her gaze bounced from one group of people to the next. Some sat in big crowds, others in fours, threes, or twos.

While she was looking at the small square tables just big enough for two, it happened. Recognition struck her as she scanned over a table with two men. Both were around the same age. Both were white, built, and had similar, chiseled faces.

Helen stilled as she realized that one was Agnes's tech assistant, Heath, and the other was Derek Green.

Chapter Ten

Agnes spent over twenty-four hours worrying about the interaction to come. The agony she'd suffered earlier when she realized Helen wasn't home, and she'd have to wait until she got back from dinner with a friend was nearly unbearable.

But Helen texted that she was home now, and Agnes raced over there, anxious to get this confrontation over with. They had to address that searing kiss they'd shared.

Helen opened the door so slowly Agnes thought the suspense might kill her. Then suddenly, they were standing face-to-face in the doorway staring into each other's eyes. Neither one moved or spoke for a long moment.

"Come in." Helen stepped aside, and Agnes squeezed through the opening. "How are you?" Helen walked, her back to Agnes, into the living room and settled carefully on the loveseat.

Despite the voice in her head warning her to stay as far away from Helen as possible, Agnes couldn't resist the urge to sit down on that cozy piece of furniture beside her. "I'm okay. How are you?"

Helen twisted up her lips in an expression Agnes hadn't quite deciphered yet. "I'm okay."

"How was dinner with your friend?" Agnes wanted to ease into the inevitable confrontation to come.

Helen's eyes shifted suddenly. Her gaze traveled around the living room. "Good. We had a nice time."

"Good. Um. I was kind of anxious to talk to you. Sorry I interrupted."

Helen's gaze finally moved back to Agnes. "It's no problem. What's on your mind?"

Agnes and Helen both knew what hung in the atmosphere between them, heavy like a thick, dark curtain blocking out the light. But Helen clearly wasn't going to be the one to initiate the conversation.

"The other night. Our kiss." Three long days had passed. Agnes would never know how she'd let it drag out this long. But tonight, the urgency of it came crashing down on her and she'd suddenly become desperate to clear the air.

Helen shifted on the loveseat, brought her leg up, and tucked it under her lap so she faced Agnes. "Did I...surprise you?"

Agnes had to recalibrate for a moment. This was not at all the direction she imagined this conversation going. But the only answer that came to mind was the truth. "Yeah."

"I surprised Jolie, too. And Malcolm. I'm not the...I'm not passive in relationships. It seems people tend to assume that."

"I assumed," Agnes admitted. "And I automatically..." She stopped herself from going full-on confession. Admitting that despite her attraction to Helen she'd written her off because she'd deduced Helen couldn't be the dominating lover she so deeply craved was a little beyond her intentions for this conversation.

Helen moved closer, her delectable lips invading Agnes's personal space. "And?"

"And...I thought...we'd never be..."

"And now?" Helen asked.

This was all getting away from Agnes. She'd come here with the intent of preventing a torrid—and surely intensely satisfying—affair, and now her mind was wandering down a path of sensuality and forbidden desires she knew she had to curb but couldn't find the will to do it.

"I'm...I'm...surprised."

Clearly disappointed with Agnes's answer, Helen leaned back. "Oh, well. I'm glad you stopped by because...because I need to tell you something."

Agnes wondered if Helen was going to beat her to the punch, delivering the delicate lecture about how they shouldn't pursue an intimate relationship. Instead, Helen completely flummoxed Agnes with her next words. "I saw Heath tonight. At the restaurant."

"Oh," was all Agnes could say, uncertain of where this was going.

"He was with..." Helen took a deep breath, and her chest expanded visibly. "He was having dinner with Derek Green."

"What?" Agnes lost all her composure. Shock was a new concept to her because she'd never experienced it quite like this.

Helen reached out a hand and encompassed Agnes's fingers in hers. "Yes. I wasn't really sure what to make of it."

Agnes's mind twisted in a jumble of confusion. She'd come to trust Heath, to think of him as her wingman. She'd kicked herself for all the wrong assumptions she made about him. She'd come to terms with her own pre-determined ideas about him and how his honesty and transparency had blown them all out of the water. And now he'd betrayed all of that, crushed it in a single act.

Gazing at Helen's apologetic expression snapped Agnes out of her intense reaction to the news she'd just been hit with. "I'll take care of Heath."

"I'm sorry," Helen said.

"Don't be sorry. You didn't do anything."

Helen's lips turned down. "I don't know. By telling you, I've created tension within your team. I feel bad about that."

Agnes mimicked Helen's position on the couch, bringing her own leg up and tucking it under her butt. She leaned toward the beautiful woman across from her. "You're always apologizing. Why is that?"

"I don't know. I guess I feel like I'm always disappointing people."

Agnes couldn't think of a single thing about Helen that was disappointing. "How so?"

"My parents wanted me to be an architect. I became a doctor."

"Hardly a deadly sin."

Helen shrugged, and her gaze fell to their interlocked fingers. "I couldn't make my marriage work. That disappointed a lot of people in both our families."

"And that was all your fault?"

Helen's eyes raised. "No. It felt like it sometimes, but it wasn't."

"And I have no doubt Malcolm would agree with that."

"What about this mess?" Helen raised her free hand and gestured listlessly before dropping it on Agnes's calf. Instead of staying limp though, she gripped Agnes's muscles in a soft, but firm, clasp using her palm and fingers. "If I hadn't dated Jolie..."

"Okay. Now you're getting ridiculous. That is no way your fault."

"It may not be my fault. Hell, none of it really is my fault. But these are things that create disappointment in the people I love."

Agnes knew gentleness would get her nowhere in this situation. "So what?"

Helen's mouth dropped open. Agnes stared at that mouth. Silence fell around them effortlessly. Agnes raised her free hand to Helen's cheek, cupping it. The kiss she gave Helen was soft and sweet. "You do the best you can. You love hard. You gotta stop taking everything on yourself."

Helen surged back toward Agnes and possessed her mouth in a searing kiss. Then she suddenly pulled back.

"That was anything but disappointing," Agnes mumbled.

Helen's smile lit up her face. "I'm sorry. You came here to tell me we shouldn't do that again, didn't you? Or that we needed to put parameters on...this...or something like that?"

"Yeah. I did." Agnes tried to think around the tingling sensation in her mouth. "But I changed my mind."

Helen cocked her head, amusement dancing on her lips. "You did, huh?"

"Yeah. Maybe we shouldn't analyze everything. You're an overthinker, and so am I. Let's...not overthink."

"I like that idea." Helen leaned toward Agnes once again.

But Agnes held her hand between them. "But, I need to deal with Heath with a clear mind. So for now, we should stop at that."

The pout that twisted Helen's lips was nearly irresistible, but somehow, Agnes managed to make it to the door.

****

"Why, exactly, are we here?" Veronica asked, her brows both raised to her hairline, a move Helen had come to recognize as a sign of "fight mode."

"We just want to go over a few more things," Detective Poll said.

Helen stared at his folded hands. They seemed too big and foreboding, resting there in the center of the table. Despite his always being kind to her, she was still appropriately afraid of him, especially with the sour-faced Detective Hillman sitting beside him, looking as though she'd just swallowed a lemon.

"What could possibly be left?" Veronica copied Poll's position, her own hands folded carefully on the table. Her massive diamond wedding ring glinted in the harsh light of the drab, little room in the back of the police station.

Detective Poll lifted a sheet of white paper from where it sat on top of a manila envelope and pretended to peruse it as if for the first time. "It's your whereabouts on the night of Jolie's death, Dr. Nims. We'd like to review that again."

Helen thought about opening her mouth to speak, but before she ever got the chance, Veronica's harsh tone echoed through the room. "Why? Has something changed since the last time Helen gave you this information in writing, or before that when she gave you the same information during an interrogation without an attorney present?"

Detective Poll seemed completely unfazed by Veronica's warlike stance. He simply smiled back at them both.

It was Detective Hillman who spoke next. "Actually, it has," she said. Not even so much as glancing at the paper Detective Poll still clutched in his hands, she stared toward Helen. The look on her face was so menacing Helen involuntarily moved back and her spine hit the hard, metal chair painfully.

"Explain," Veronica said.

Detective Hillman clearly wasn't about to explain anything. "I'd rather hear your client walk us through that night again." Her lips were pursed so tightly Helen wondered if permanent shrinkage might occur.

Helen took in a deep breath and exhaled slowly. She placed her hand on Veronica's arm. "What time frame do you want me to review?"

"Ten o'clock until eleven-thirty," Detective Hillman said with no emotion.

"I was charting at the hospital until around midnight." Helen had been through this a million times. She had no idea why they were bringing this up again.

"There are witnesses," Veronica added.

"Well that's the issue." Detective Poll pushed his thick, black-rimmed glasses up on his nose. "One of your witnesses has recanted, and another has decided she's not so sure."

Helen was thrown out of orbit, her mind reeling. No way had James changed his defiant insistence that he'd spoken to her on three separate occasions during that timespan. That left two people she thought were her friends—or at least her friendly coworkers.

"We're going to need details," Veronica said, her arms folded over her chest, lips firm, eyes hooded. She was pissed, and Helen felt bad for Detective Poll to have to stare her down.

"Doctor Tombie now says he didn't see you in the chart room after ten o'clock that night." Detective Poll glanced briefly at the sheet of paper in front of him before looking back up at Helen.

Helen's eyes nearly popped out of her head. Elliot Tombie sat at the little charting desk beside her for at least half an hour during that time. They'd discussed their surgeries, and he'd even offered her a chocolate chip cookie his wife had made, from a plastic container with a purple top.

"That's not true," she said, her voice soft and weak. "He was there, in the chart room."

"Well, he says you weren't."

Helen's heart hurt. Why would someone lie about that? Especially a colleague. "I don't understand."

Veronica held her hand up in front of Helen. "And the other person?"

"A nurse, Janis Allen. She originally said she brought Dr. Nims her charts that night. But now she says she doesn't remember. She thinks she might have mixed up the nights."

"But the charts are signed and dated!" Helen protested.

Veronica held up her hand again. Helen slumped back in her chair. But Veronica repeated the protest. "The charts are signed and dated. Did you look at them?"

"We did," Detective Poll said. "But we need proof that the date and time are genuine. It would be easy to fake."

Helen was speechless. Never had she been accused of faking a chart, let alone to cover up for a murder. But that's exactly what was being suggested.

"Is my client under arrest?" Veronica's words were, perhaps, the most alarming ones Helen had ever heard in her life.

"No," Detective Poll said.

"Then we're leaving." Veronica stood. "I suggest you give your witnesses lie detector tests."

Chapter Eleven

You think you know someone. The phrase ran through Agnes's brain again and again as she stalked toward the conference room, Heath at her heels. Once they were both inside, she slammed the door shut. She grabbed the string to the blinds on the internal windows, yanked on it, and let the plastic verticals drop with a loud clank. She spun on the heel of her practical black flats and pierced Heath with a laser gaze.

Heath looked like a sweet puppy who'd just been caught chewing up $200 shoes. His wide blue eyes nearly strained out of his head. His flushed cheeks told her he knew she was pissed.

"Spill. Now." She stalked toward him until he was pinned against the oak table that pressed against the place where his thighs and ass met.

"I'm guessing this is about Derek Green." Despite his precarious situation, Heath was still far too calm. "I saw Helen at the restaurant. I planned to tell you—"

"Oh really. Because you could have called last night."

"I was about to ask you to go to coffee with me, so I could explain the whole thing, when you shoved me in here." His tone was still bright and cheery, only further stoking Agnes's anger. But he betrayed his cool by running one hand through his hair, carelessly ruffling the usually well-coifed do. "You still wanna get that coffee?"

"If I decide not to kill you. Tell it first," Agnes said.

"We want an interview with Derek, right? I mean, you want an interview."

A pinprick of guilt hit Agnes in the gut. She'd come to think of Heath and herself as a team, and he obviously had, too—until she'd turned on him. But at this point, she didn't have enough information to know whether or not he deserved that betrayal. So she simply nodded.

"Right. So I thought I'd try. I know this guy. I knew a dozen guys like Derek in college. I played ball with guys like him all through high school. Hell, I still bowl with a couple of classic Dereks. I know how to speak his language."

Without a mirror, she knew the expression on her face was one of confusion because Heath launched into an explanation. "He doesn't trust women, at least not smart, hard-ass women like you. There's no way in hell he's ever going to answer your calls. But a fraternity brother—he'd take a call from a brother for sure."

Agnes's jaw dropped so hard a slight ache accompanied the involuntary action. "You know him?"

"I don't know him. We were part of the same frat, at different schools, different times. But that doesn't matter. A brother is a brother."

Agnes swiveled a chair around and fell into it. "How long have you known this? Why didn't you say anything?" She'd thought of them as partners; the betrayal she felt now was proof of that.

"I just found out last night when I was doing some digging on his social media. I called him immediately. He agreed to talk over drinks. I didn't think, Agnes, I just went. I didn't want to hesitate or scare him off."

Agnes nodded slowly. That all made sense. She'd do the same thing, knowing she had to act instinctively and quickly, with plans to catch Heath up later. "Okay. So what did you talk about?"

Heath pulled out a chair and turned it to face her before sliding into it. "Frat stuff. Guy stuff."

There was no stopping her eyes from doing a complete and thorough roll. It didn't go unnoticed.

Heath let out a heavy breath. "Like stupid shit, you know? We talked about where we went to school and what the frat brothers were like there. Shit like that. A lot of it was pretty misogynistic. And while I don't roll with that stuff since I got with Barbara, and she kicked my ass into gear over women's rights, I played along. That dude is a real douche bag. He hates women."

Suddenly, all her irritation was replaced with pure curiosity. "And...did he say anything about Jolie?"

"I didn't go there, yet. I'm trying to gain his trust. Build up. I set up another meeting with him on Saturday."

Agnes's spine straightened. "I want to go."

Heath shot out of his chair and towered over her at his full height. "No. Agnes, I gotta gain his trust first. That's not going to happen if you're there."

They stared at each other for a long, hard moment. Then Heath said something she couldn't find the will to respond to. "You've got to trust me."

****

What led to this moment was still unclear in Helen's muddle mind. Her brain whirled a mile a minute and insisted she take action to save herself. That led to picking up her cell and dialing a number she thought she'd never need again.

"Weddings Best Friend is no longer in business. Can I direct your call somewhere else?" The woman working at the answering service sounded as if she'd said the phrase a million times in the past few days.

"Hi. I'm a client and I still need to pay my bill. How does that work?"

"Oh. Yeah. You can pay Mr. Green. Just a moment." Helen held her breath as soothing hold music accompanied her anxiety.

"Ma'am, are you still there?"

"Yes. I am."

"You can arrange payment directly with Mr. Green. Let me give you his number."

Understanding Derek's greed had led Helen directly to the man himself. Five minutes later, Helen had him on the phone.

"Yeah?"

"Is this Derek?"

"Who wants to know?"

"Helen." She let it sit there for a moment. The word—

her name—lingered on the phone line between them.

His voice was deeper, gruffer when he spoke again. "What do you want?"

"I want you to tell the truth. What happened the night Jolie died?"

Silence blanketed them. A low buzz over the line was all she heard. For a moment, Helen wondered if he'd actually do it. Then he laughed. The sound of it sent chills through her body. As the blood drained from her face, she hit the bright-red Phone symbol and hung up on him, effectively ending the conversation.

But her action only increased her anxiety. Worse, it fueled her anger. With adrenaline coursing through her, she marveled at how still every part of her body had suddenly become.

Her hands didn't shake as she pulled the keys from the small, square table where they lay. She tucked Kimber into her elbow, grabbed the small doggie bag of supplies, marched to her rarely used sedan, pulled up her map app, and prepared for the short, traffic-gnarled trip to Potrero Hill.

The surprise painted on Agnes's face when she opened the door gave Helen pause. The enthusiastic greeting she received from Jasper was a bit different. As he jumped up and whined, Kimber squirmed in her arms. Agnes ushered her in, and she dropped her bag and gently placed Kimber on the floor of the small entryway. Both women watched with amusement as the big mutt was quickly schooled on the pecking order by the tiny poodle. The dogs trotted off to the kitchen, and the women were left alone.

Thick carpeting cushioned Helen's steps as she moved into the living room. The white walls of the apartment were covered in artwork, abstract pieces with dancing women in flowing robes or cubist faces peering out above low walls. Helen made her way to the dark-brown, leather sofa and sunk into it without invitation.

"Is everything all right?" Agnes followed her into the living room but stopped a few feet in front of her. Hands hanging at her sides, she cocked her head.

"I had a bad day."

Agnes let out a long breath as she sat heavily on the couch beside her. "Me, too."

"Do you want to talk about it?" Helen asked.

Agnes shook her head. "You?"

"No." Helen rested her head against the back of the couch. "Why is everything so hard?" Agnes's soft hand landed on her thigh and sent heat radiating into her core. Helen kept her eyes on the ceiling. "I actually came over here to see if you want to come with me to Derek's house to beat him up."

Agnes's voice was like a soothing cup of tea, taking the sting of tears out of Helen's eyes. "Why are we beating him up, exactly? I mean, I'm pretty sure there are a lot of reasons, but we need to have our stories straight, you know."

Despite her words of action, Helen sank farther into the couch and listed ever so slightly toward Agnes. "To beat the truth out of him about what happened to Jolie." Her voice grew softer even as she leaned over and rested her shoulder against Agnes, bringing their faces close. "I want him to stop implying I hurt her. I wouldn't do that. I couldn't."

The threatening tears were set loose by a gentle stroke from Agnes. "I know, sweetheart. Everyone who knows you knows that."

Helen shook her head, speech now beyond her. She couldn't help but think about the coworkers she'd seen everyday, shared coffee with, laughed with. They didn't know her. They'd turned on her.

"Hey," Agnes whispered as her lips pressed gently against Helen's cheek. "You just have to ride this out. It's going to be okay. I promise."

Helen lifted her head so their noses were nearly touching. Her dark eyes bored into Agnes's lighter ones. "You promise?"

Agnes nodded slowly. "I'll do everything in my power to make it okay again."

Words floated in Helen's head, but she didn't let any of them loose. Instead, she closed the distance between her and Agnes and placed her lips against Agnes's soft, pliant ones.

Sweet and gentle quickly turned to hot and urgent. Unable to resist the desire burning through her, Helen rose up on her knees and guided Agnes back against the seat of the couch. One leg wedged between Agnes's slender hip and the couch back, the other between Agnes's knees.

Agnes let out a low moan. Helen couldn't resist pulling her lips back to give the other woman a smile. Her hand slid down Agnes's stomach, which arched in response to her touch.

Helen placed another soft kiss on Agnes's lips before pulling back again to watch as she shimmied the soft, cotton leggings down until they hit the place where all three knees met. Then Helen slipped her fingers inside Agnes's silky panties. Her eyes never left Agnes's face as it shifted back, chin reaching toward the ceiling. As Helen's fingers sank into the heaven that was Agnes, Agnes's lips formed an ellipse of ecstasy.

The moment froze for Helen, even as her body continued to move. Lips trailed down Agnes's neck. Her other hand tugged at clothing. Her fingers worked their magic, pulling moans and gasps from Agnes. But even while all that was happening, Helen took a mental snapshot of that first moment she and Agnes had come together.

As Agnes's cries began to calm, and her orgasm turned from frenzy to satisfied aftermath, she leaned forward to Helen's ear and said one word. "Stay."

Chapter Twelve

"We have to talk." Agnes tried not to slam the door to Nils's office, but it still snapped shut with an audible clap. When she spun back around, Nils closed his laptop and peered up at her with feigned patience.

"Have a seat." He pointed to one of the two chairs that sat opposite him, the large imposing desk between them setting apart boss from employee.

"You're calm," she said.

"Yep."

Alarm overwhelmed her. Nils held a constant-motion, high-stress job. He was never relaxed like this, unless he knew he had a killer lead on a story. That had happened a few times. She took a split second to wonder who'd gotten the scoop of a lifetime before bringing herself back to the present.

"I need you to take me off the Jolie Green story." She straightened her back and kept her expression neutral.

She expected a lot of things—a jaw wrenched open in disbelief, a hair-pulling fit, or maybe a firmly shaken head—instead Nils simply smiled and said, "No."

Agnes met his calm with her own. "Let me explain. Last night I slept with Helen Nims. I broke every rule. I totally screwed up. You should probably fire me, though of course I hope you don't. I hope you'll just reassign me and give me a reprimand." The practiced speech flowed out of her much faster and earlier in the conversation than she'd intended.

"You have a girlfriend?" His eyes lit up with delight.

It was Agnes's jaw that dropped. "That's what you have to say?"

"I like my staff to have fulfilling and healthy love lives."

"With an interviewee?" she practically shouted.

Nils shrugged. Helen knew there had to be a big story on the docket. He'd never be this relaxed otherwise.

"You don't find that problematic?"

"Is she the killer?"

"No!"

Nils shrugged again. "Then so what?"

There was a long silence as they stared at each other, Agnes with a wide-open mouth. Jaw aching, she finally closed it and glared at him. He stared back.

"Don't you think this is a conflict of interest?"

Finally Nils moved out of his "statue in repose" impersonation and stretched his clasped hands across the massive desk as if he were trying to master an awkward Yoga pose. "I'm not really worried about you, Agnes. I don't think your actions are going to end in a lawsuit or a skewed story. In fact, lover or not, I suspect you'd be the first one to call it in if she gave you a bedside confession. No. I don't care. Have fun. Be happy. And get this story. Because it's going to be good."

Agnes huffed out a breath. This was not at all going how she'd predicted. All that time wasted on her angst and worry, and she wasn't even cut from the story. Even though she didn't actually want to be taken off it, she felt compelled to give it one more try for the sake of ethics. "I think Heath might be doing some things that are questionable."

Nils's lips curled, and his gleaming teeth became the most prominent feature on his face. "I know."

"You know?" This early morning meeting was taking one crazy turn after another.

Nils hit a button on his phone and made a command into it. "Jack, bring me Heath." He didn't wait for a response, just clicked it off and turned back to her. "Did you see the numbers on the podcast launch? We just put out the trailer, and people are already buzzing about it."

She and Heath had put together three full episodes, but with no clue where the story was going next, they'd been hesitant to pick a launch date. Nils didn't care about that. He'd put out a trailer with no date attached just to see what the response was. Now that it was positive, Agnes knew it would place pressure on her and Heath to pick a launch date soon and get more episodes put together—that in essence meant pressure to solve this crime.

"Look, Nils. I'm not a police detective. In fact, I haven't made any inroads with the police. They won't tell me shit. Which is unusual. I'm not in a position to—"

The door Agnes had shut ten minutes before flung open.

"Heath! Just the man I wanted to see."

Heath bounded into the room and dropped casually into the chair beside her. Despite his demeanor, Heath had a distinctive look of guilt on his face as he looked briefly at Agnes before turning his full attention to their boss.

"Heath and I have a plan. And before you start feeling left out"—Nils held up his hand—"we tried to call you last night to conference with us about it, but you weren't answering your phone. So we planned to tell you this morning, and here we are."

Agnes had to push away the memory of what she'd been doing at the moment the phone had rung. A brief flash of herself face down on the pillow, ass in the air, legs spread, and Helen... She'd ignored the phone.

Agnes took a deep breath and reset herself. "Okay. Tell me what's going on."

"Heath is going to hang out with Derek again, and he's going to wear a wire." Nils clapped his hands together as if he'd just announced the winner of a trophy. In Agnes's mind, the prize would denote the dumbest idea ever.

"What the hell?" She turned to face Heath, who looked at her with red cheeks and wide eyes.

"You don't like it." Heath said it as a statement, not a question.

"Are you crazy? This guy could be a murderer, and you're going to hang out with him with a wire on?"

Heath shrugged. "I wanna get him, Agnes. Don't you?"

"Of course, I do! But I don't need a dead partner in the process."

"You're overreacting," Nils said. "It will be perfectly safe."

Agnes narrowed her eyes. "O-kay," she said slowly. "So this meeting will take place in a public place?"

"Nah. I'm going to hang out at his place and play pool," Heath said casually.

"What?"

The pitch of her voice must have been threatening, because Heath held his hands up in the air as if he were being arrested. "Well, I can't get him to talk about murdering his wife in the middle of a bar, now can I?"

Agnes turned back to Nils. Surely he would see that this crackpot idea was unnecessarily dangerous. At the very least, he'd be concerned about the insurance rates going up if an employee got murdered and dismembered by a psycho killer.

"The police are involved," Nils said calmly.

While not unheard of in their world, it was pretty rare for them to involve the police before they got any information, mostly because the police wanted them to stay away from dangerous suspects. Sometimes, they would gather a discarded straw or cigarette butt, have it tested, and hand it all over to the police. But a wire, a setup—this all felt very different.

"Wait. They're going along with this?"

Nils nodded. "They won't talk about an open investigation, of course."

Agnes knew this all too well. She'd been getting that line since this all started over a month ago.

"But," Nils said, "when I presented this opportunity, they jumped at the chance. It's not that different from the online pedophile sting we did two years ago."

"Really? Because there was a fake house full of like ten people, including cops, that we lured one sicko at a time to. This is Heath going into a killer's house alone." Agnes was stuck on Heath's safety, and she couldn't figure out why she was the only one who seemed to care about it.

"It'll be okay." Heath shifted in his seat. "A van with police officers will listen to everything that's said, and more cops on stand-by will come save my ass or arrest the guy or whatever goes down. It'll be like in the movies."

Agnes said, "Except this isn't the movies."

Heath put his hand over hers. In that moment, Agnes realized she trusted Heath and his motives. They'd gone from resentful strangers to misunderstood acquaintances, to cautious friends, to partners. She cared about Heath. She was invested in his safety, just as she was invested in Helen's. Taken altogether, it made her want to run as far away from the entire situation surrounding Jolie's death as she could and take the people she cared for with her.

Agnes pulled her hand away from Heath's, rubbed it over her forehead, and tried to smooth the worry wrinkles there. "So this is really going down, then?" Both men nodded. They looked like kids excited to play cops and robbers in the backyard. "When?"

"Don't know, yet. Derek invited me at the bar last night, but we didn't make it a solid thing. I didn't want to push and sound fishy, ya know? He did say he was super busy with work right now. He works in his family's electronics business. Which was totally another thing we had in common. Anyway, he said he'd call me when he was feeling less overwhelmed."

Agnes ran a hand through her hair before standing abruptly. There was still a chance Derek would never call and invite Heath into his murder basement to play pool. "Fine. If I'm still on this story, I have work to do."

****

When she split with Malcolm, Helen insisted he keep the massive California King bed they bought together in their first year of marriage. She didn't regret that decision one bit as the queen bed she now owned brought Agnes's perfect body close to her own.

Light streamed into the room through the thin rectangle of space between the blinds and the windowsill and provided Helen with the opportunity to gaze at Agnes's face. A lock of rich, brown hair draped across her neck. Long lashes kissed the tops of high cheeks, and soft, kissable lips were slightly parted and inviting. Four incredible nights with Agnes in this bed had only made the magic of waking up to her that much more potent.

Agnes stretched one arm over her head before dropping it over Helen's waist. "Hey."

Helen gently brushed the lock of hair away and stared into the now open eyes of the woman she'd taken so much comfort in for the past two weeks. "Good morning."

"Hey, baby." Agnes pulled herself up and planted a soft kiss on Helen's waiting lips. "Have you been awake long?"

"Not long."

Agnes rested her cheek on her wrist and frowned down at Helen. "Have you been worrying all night again?"

Unable to lie to that face, Helen exhaled and squeezed her eyes closed for a moment before looking back into Agnes's concern-filled face. "Not all night."

Agnes ran her finger down Helen's cheek, the gentle touch far more soothing than she could possibly know. "Okay. What's at the top of your worry list?"

"That I might go to jail for killing my girlfriend—that I totally didn't do, by the way."

"I know that." Agnes planted a soft kiss on Helen's nose. "And I won't let that happen. Not to mention Malcolm or Veronica. God forbid anyone fuck with Veronica. What's number two?"

"That I might lose my job." Helen peered up at Agnes. She tried desperately to convey her fears in that look. "I still can't believe I got put on administrative leave."

The call from James the night before set her on a terrible spiral that even an intense session of lovemaking with Agnes couldn't completely quell. His voice cracked in pain as he delivered the news that the hospital administration had decided to put her on paid leave indefinitely.

"I might lose my job, too," Agnes said. "Then we can stay home in bed all day. Maybe we should get another dog." Helen couldn't resist the light chuckle that escaped her. Kimber and Jasper were currently curled up in the corner of the room, sharing one bed and snoring loudly.

Agnes always had a way of lightening her mood. That thought was followed by another, which she voiced. "Do you think it's bad that we got together in the midst of all this stress?"

Agnes's lips turned down then up again as she thought about that, and her hand made a trail across Helen's neck over and over. "I think you're overthinking it."

Every muscle in Helen's body tensed. That was something she once said to Jolie when she wanted to get out of the more serious relationship Jolie was pushing. Was that what was happening now? Was Agnes pulling away?

Their stint as a couple had been incredibly short, but already Helen felt an irresistible pull toward Agnes. She anticipated their time together in a way she hadn't ever experienced. Agnes had quickly become the first person she wanted to talk to when anything happened in her day.

As if she were a puzzle piece, Agnes fit into Helen's life despite the chaos it had been thrown into recently. She didn't mind Helen's closeness with Malcolm, in fact she respected and encouraged it. She'd gone with Helen to a bar to meet James and his wife, and she'd blended perfectly at the Sunday barbeque at Malcolm's mom's house.

Perhaps most important, they circled around each other like planets of equal gravitation. Helen didn't feel like a satellite floating around a brighter, shinier star like she had with Jolie. Nor did she feel like the dominating planet, overshadowing a moon she wished to be less passive, like she did with Malcolm.

But the jarring idea that her own feelings might be out of line with Agnes was taking over her thoughts. It moved like a well-aimed dart to her heart. "Okay." The urge to flee overwhelmed Helen. She couldn't deal with this barrage of feelings in front of Agnes. So she slid toward the side of the bed, extricated herself from the other woman, and focused her eyes on the floor beside her.

"Where are you going?" Agnes asked. "What happened?"

Agnes's instant awareness that something was wrong and Helen wasn't just headed to the bathroom had her snap her head to the side. Agnes sat up, hands reached toward Helen, eyes wide.

Helen slumped back into the bed and rested her back against the headboard. "I'm having a moment," she admitted.

Agnes scooted closer to her and placed a hand on her

shoulder. "Tell me about it."

Helen's shallow breaths told her she was about to do something stupid. The fear and anxiety that manifested in low breaths and a thumping heart had been followed by a perfectly executed surgical cut hundreds of times. Now it was prefacing a single, fateful statement. "I want this to be more. I'm really, really attached to you already, and I want more."

Agnes sighed. "I've heard that before, you know. It's when I usually run."

Helen's heart squeezed. She suspected as much.

"I've always been this way. I don't feel like I have the ability to do more. I prefer the no-strings thing. Usually on the first date, I give a whole lecture about it." Agnes smiled weakly. It did nothing to calm Helen's racing mind. "But I didn't give you that lecture."

Helen shook her head, holding back tears. She wished Agnes had, then she wouldn't be here about to have her heart split in two.

"Because it doesn't apply to you."

"What do you mean?"

"I mean"—Agnes ran a hand lightly over Helen's cheek—"I want more, too."

Chapter Thirteen

It had been two years since Agnes had taken a four-day weekend. Having given up on any relationship being fulfilling enough, she'd immersed herself in her work. Helen had changed all that.

"I've never been to a timeshare before." Agnes dropped her bag on the luggage rack just inside the master bedroom. She wandered out to the balcony that overlooked the sparkling pool. "It's like a rental house."

"Basically, yes. I thought it was a dumb idea when Malcolm's parents bought it. But now I see the point. Lots of choices, different destinations." Helen dumped her own suitcase on the floor, walked up behind Agnes, and wrapped her arms around her waist. "I like this particular spot a lot."

"Have you been here before, with Malcolm?"

Helen rested her chin on Agnes's shoulder. Her thumb ran up and down over a sensitive spot on her hip. "Actually, yes. We came here once while we were married." Helen stood straight and turned Agnes around to face her. "Is that a problem?" She frowned. "We can get a hotel. Or find a—"

Agnes put her finger over Helen's lips. "No. It's okay."

Helen tilted her head. "It is?"

"Except for one thing. We're not sleeping on that bed." She pointed to the massive king-size bed, with a little remorse. One of the two guest rooms would have to do.

Helen laughed. "Well, that's where Malcolm's parents slept. We stayed in one of the other rooms."

"Oh."

Helen smiled. "It was a family trip. There wasn't any hanky panky."

Agnes kissed Helen playfully. "Okay then. This room it is."

"I know you love wine as much as I do. I have to say,

this trip will be more fun with you than with them." She released Agnes, went to the French doors, and opened them up to the warm, dry air of Napa Valley.

"I've only visited here on a bus with a bunch of rowdy women."

"Are you saying I'm not rowdy?" Helen asked, innocent look on full display as she turned back to Agnes and stalked toward her.

"Rowdy?" Agnes placed a finger on her chin as if to contemplate this question. "Not you." She shook her head.

Helen pounced, pushed Agnes onto the bed, and climbed over her. "You sure about that?"

It was so good to see Helen being playful and carefree, Agnes couldn't suppress the massive grin that split her mouth from ear to ear. Meeting in the middle of her partner's life imploding meant she had missed all the fun and laughter that usually came with the beginning of a relationship, but Agnes hadn't noticed until that moment.

She pressed her lips to Helen's and snuck a hand under her flowing, linen dress. "Hmm. Why don't you show me how rowdy you are?"

Helen grabbed Agnes's wrists and pulled them over her head, pressing them in to the mattress. Then she straddled Agnes's hips and looked down at her with a hungry expression. "Oh, I will."

As Helen began a slow and tortuous route with her tongue that began at Agnes's chin and went all the way to the top of her V-neck. Agnes found a tiny spot in her brain with the capacity to realize that this trip—four days in wine country, touring cellars, hiking, and eating at high-end restaurants—was exactly what they needed.

She'd suggested a vacation the morning after Helen admitted that she wanted more in their relationship. Agnes was jolted to her core by that conversation. Unlike Helen, she'd become accustomed to living life in the moment. After all, how could she plan for something down the line when a big story might drop in her lap, and she'd have to travel to the far northern region of the state for three weeks to work on it? How could she conceive of what might happen with a date three months from now when she wasn't sure she'd find the time to spend more than a few hours a week with that person between now and then?

But a work/life balance had been achieved by several of her colleagues. She'd even had occasion to discuss with her old therapist how she hid behind that excuse to prevent intimacy. But still, she used that excuse.

Only she'd completely forgotten it the first time Helen spent the night in her arms. She'd forgotten that her fear of getting hurt had created such a high wall around her heart no one had been able to scale it. She'd forgotten that she needed to keep every lover at arm's length and quash the super attachment so many women in her life seemed inclined to display.

She'd forgotten all of it, because she had recklessly fallen in love with Dr. Helen Nims.

****

"Put your foot down," Helen growled. The laughter bubbling in her throat was barely disguised by her fake anger.

Despite the slapping hand, Agnes raised her barefoot back up and dropped it again on Helen's knee. Her body lay perpendicular to Helen's, her perfect figure sprawled across the couch in utter relaxation, glass of wine held haphazardly in one hand while the other waved around chaotically as she talked.

Helen sat on the other end of the couch, feet propped on the coffee table, also in perfect repose, full wineglass in hand. "You're a pest."

"You love me," Agnes said.

No amount of Napa Valley's finest red wine could have allowed them to move past that moment. It froze in time and hung in the air between them like an icicle about to drop from a great height, the anticipation of the break and shatter that was to come a combination of terror and beauty.

Three days had changed everything between them. They would leave this place in the morning, head back to the city, sleep off the excess wine, and get up to go to work on Tuesday. Well, Agnes would go to work. Helen would go to the free clinic to volunteer her time.

But now, in the safety of their little, three-bedroom cottage on the edge of a field filled with grapevines and sunshine, they were in a place like Helen had never been before. It was all so surreal. Every moment with Agnes was like a homecoming. Even their arguments were pieces of the puzzle. When one wanted to head in one direction and the other in the opposite, they somehow agreed in the end. The winner bounced back and forth like a memorandum of understanding that when Helen got her way Agnes would next time and vice versa.

Never had it been so easy.

And all this was happening in the midst of the worst time in Helen's life. When everything was falling apart— her job, her friendships, even her freedom were all on the line—she'd found an incredible sense of peace with Agnes.

In the beginning, Helen feared that Agnes would run from commitment, so she locked all her own feelings away, choosing time with Agnes over her own heart. All that was forgotten over the past three days. They were more like a happily married couple than a new, casual fling. Agnes's lecture to her past lovers seemed a million miles and a hundred years away.

But it rushed to the forefront now as those words hung in the air. That word. The truth beat on her cheeks inside her tightly closed mouth, begging to be set free. With just a split second to decide, Helen chose heartache over the façade. "I do."

There was another long moment. Agnes didn't move. Helen wasn't sure she was even breathing. Then, suddenly, she popped up and her legs swung away from Helen as her torso flew toward her. Agnes placed her hands on either side of Helen's face and stared into her eyes.

"Me, too. Me, too." Then she began to kiss Helen with a fury the passive Agnes never used in lovemaking.

Helen kissed her back, quickly regaining control. She pulled Agnes onto her lap, legs to one side. Mouth still planted firmly to Agnes's lips, she wrenched down the cotton shorts

Agnes wore and tossed them into the universe somewhere. The panties went as well before she lifted one of Agnes's legs and pulled it over her lap.

With Agnes straddling her, Helen leaned farther back in the couch, using a firm hand on Agnes's back to pull her with her. She kissed Agnes with fire and passion, tangling their tongues together, occasionally gnashing teeth.

All the while, her hands moved with focus and intent. While one stayed on Agnes's lower back, the other moved between her thighs. Two fingers slipped inside, while her nimble thumb went to work.

Helen's surgeon's hands were meant for this—to make her lover squirm and scream. Agnes arched her back, pulled her mouth free. Her neck formed a beautiful curve in front of Helen's face, and she cried out. Her body shook with her orgasm.

Helen was whole.

Chapter Fourteen

Arriving back at her apartment alone on Monday night felt to Agnes like coming down from a mountain to a dark, sunless valley. Not even Jasper was there to greet her, as he and Kimber were both still at the kennel in the East Bay. Helen would pick them up tomorrow.

Helen. The long weekend with Helen had been magical. Not only had it been a much-needed break for Helen from her stress and for Agnes from her work, but they had thoroughly enjoyed one another.

They'd confessed their feelings and taken their relationship to the next level. An unexpected surprise, one Agnes still reveled in twenty-four hours later. The anxiety and claustrophobic reflex that usually accompanied any conversation of long-term commitment was conspicuously absent.

Agnes dropped her bag at the edge of the living room and looked around. Her place was tidy and clean, thanks to Helen, who'd scrubbed it top to bottom last time she was here. Agnes had no clue where anything was. The book she kept picking up and putting down that lived on a pile of old mail; her small collection of empty plastic containers that sat in one corner of the kitchen counter waiting for a purpose; and the jumble of rubber bands, staple rows, and paperclips that were strewn across her end table like a beached fishing net were all gone. She didn't miss them at all. What she missed was Helen.

Agnes pulled her phone out of her pocket, fully intent on texting Helen to see if she wanted company. Forget that it was Agnes who suggested they spend the night apart so she could focus on work and be ready for the morning meeting on Tuesday. She needed Helen more than she needed time with her computer.

She'd just pulled up the messaging when the phone

rang. Heath's face appeared on the screen as the song he often hummed indicated his call.

Agnes's throat tightened as she answered. She didn't know why, but something was wrong. "Heath."

"Hey." Heath's voice, in that short syllable betrayed him. Something *was* wrong. "I, um, I'm getting ready. Can you come over?"

"What are you talking about? Getting ready for what?"

"I'm hanging out with Derek in an hour, at his place, alone."

Agnes didn't waste a moment. She hung up and raced to her seldom-used car. She drove the dusty thing out of the garage she rented for exorbitant rates and headed to North Beach.

By the time she got through the snarling Monday evening traffic and, like a needle in a haystack, finally located a street-side parking spot, she'd wasted nearly forty minutes. The bus would have taken just as long.

Throwing her frustration aside, Agnes leaped up the stone steps she'd seen Heath take after dropping him off but had never been up herself. It was Nils who met her at the door. He was calm and collected, as were the three other people there, two producers and a fellow tech guy who had been around a lot longer than Heath and served as his mentor. Heath, however, looked as frantic as she felt.

"Where are the police?" she asked the minute she entered the spacious living room where Frank was sticking something into Heath's pants pocket.

"They're prepared to accept the tape after we get it."

"But they're not here?"

"It's okay, Agnes," Heath said, his blue eyes wide. "I got this."

"You're going into a house—alone—with a murderer. I don't think you got this."

"I thought we didn't know if he was a murderer yet."

Agnes turned around to see Molly, a newer producer who came to them from what Agnes considered a much-less-credible and much-sleazier crime show. She had her hand on her hip and a challenge in her eye.

"Technically, no. But he's a suspect."

"Person of interest," Molly shot back.

To stem an explosion of anger, Agnes simply turned her back on the woman and tried to clear her gaze as she pulled it toward Heath. "You're a mess. Look at you." Her arm ran up and down showcasing his basketball shorts and slightly wrinkled, sports-logo T-shirt. While that might be appropriate for a night of bro-ing around, the wide blood-shot eyes, sweaty forehead, and disheveled head of hair showed a man under extreme stress. "Don't you think he's going to know something's up?"

"I told him I was up all night over a girl. That's why he invited me over, to commiserate. It's the perfect setup to get him talking about his ex-wife, don't you think?"

Agnes sighed. It was a good idea. But it did nothing to ease her fear. "What if he pats you down?"

"No worries," Frank said. He pulled something out of Heath's baggy front pocket, producing a small cell phone. "It's not weird to have two phones. This one will not only broadcast but record the whole thing without even looking like it's on." He slipped the phone back in Heath's pocket and put his paw on Agnes's shoulder. "We do this all the time, Agnes. Chill."

Agnes pivoted so Frank's hand fell off her. She stepped toward Heath. She touched her fingers to his cheek and stared into his eyes. It might look romantic to onlookers, but she didn't care. She knew what it was and so did Heath. It was sisterly. That's what it was.

"Be careful."

Heath nodded.

"If you get murdered, I'm gonna kill you."

Heath chuckled, which was exactly what they both needed. So Agnes slapped him lightly on the check, swallowed the lump in her throat, and walked away.

****

The heavy headphone set yanked on Agnes's ears. A random memory of Heath tugging one lobe and telling her how tiny it was skittered into her brain, bringing with it a shiver of terror that was accompanied by Heath's voice.

"Yeah, it sucks so bad, man. I mean, I gave her every-thing, you know? And she's not only leaving me, she says she's gonna get a lawyer and get money out of me, too. We weren't even married."

"The best thing you ever did was not to marry the bitch." Derek's voice, cold and evil, hit Agnes in the stomach. She hated that Heath was alone with this guy.

The sound of billiard balls clashing together rang out over the line. When they went silent, Heath spoke again. "Tell me about it. She was always pushing for it. I'm glad as hell I never gave in. How the hell did you get trapped?"

Derek pushed out a deep laugh. "Man, I don't even know any more."

"Were you glad to get divorced?"

Agnes drew in a deep breath. This was where the last two hours of beers, pool, and stupid banter had led them. This was the crucial moment.

The silence that greeted Heath's question vibrated over the transmission, accompanied only by quiet white noise. Until finally, Derek spoke. "Have you seen my ex? She's fucking hot as hell. I was not done with that yet, man. No, I told her to take her divorce and shove it. But she wouldn't fucking listen. She was too interested in getting her hands on my money."

"No shit? She robbed you, eh?"

Derek's voice took on a new urgency, as if he were sud-denly desperate to download his story. "Yeah. So check this out. My parents put her in charge of my trust fund when we got married. And when we got divorced, she gave it back to them instead of me. And I fucking guarantee that my dad offered her a kickback to do it."

Agnes realized in that moment that Heath was a genius. He probably should have been a detective. At the very least, he should be given a shot at reporter for the show.

Derek's simmering anger continued to climb. "All she had to do was sign it over to me. I practically begged the bitch to do it."

"I think I would fucking kill over that."

Breath trapped under the weight of her crushing anxiety, Agnes waited to hear if Derek would take the bait Heath just offered him."

"Would you?" Derek asked. "Seriously?"

"If I could figure out how to get away with it."

"And, uh, how would you do it? I mean, how would you get away with it?"

Heath paused for a moment. The recording device disguised as a phone in his pocket was so sensitive it picked up the scratching of the scruff on his chin as he rubbed it with something. Agnes wished like hell they had figured out how to get video as well so she could gauge the feel in that room. Was Heath in danger?

"I would get a scapegoat to frame first of all," Heath said. "I mean, the rest of the details all depend on that, right?"

"What kind of scapegoat?"

"An ex-lover." Heath said. "Or a current one. Like that guy Shelly left me for. I'd frame that son-of-a-bitch for her murder."

Another painful pause elongated the suspense. Then Derek changed the whole game. "That's exactly what I did."

****

As soon as she'd received the text that asked if Agnes could spend the night, Helen began to anticipate her arrival. The second text, that Agnes would be late because of something with work and was it still okay, had only made the ache stronger.

Helen puttered around her house, heated up some tea, tidied the bedroom, put some clothes in the washer. She didn't mind staying up—she had no job to go to after all— but she did hate the wait.

The irresistible pull of Agnes was undeniable. Helen only hoped it wasn't also unwelcomed. She was attempting to pull herself out of that spiral of negative thought when Agnes arrived.

"I'm sorry it's so late." She planted a quick kiss on Helen's cheek and moved into the living room.

"Is everything okay?"

Agnes slumped down on the couch. She looked exhausted to the core. "Perfect, actually." Despite her obvious fatigue, a wide grin split her face.

Helen approached slowly. Her movements reflected the speed of the wheels that turned in her head. What did all this mean? The only thing Agnes was working on was Jolie's case. What could be perfect?

She settled on the couch beside Agnes, one hand immediately landing on her thigh. "What's perfect?"

Agnes planted another enthusiastic peck on her cheek and moved back to beam at her. "We got him."

The room seemed to spin as Helen tried to grab hold of what Agnes was saying. "What?"

"Heath recorded Derek Green tonight, confessing to Jolie's murder."

Helen's muddled mind reeled. "What?"

Agnes shifted on the couch. She kicked off her shoes and pulled one leg up so she faced Helen. The excitement in her bright eyes shone like twin lights. "I thought it was crazy dangerous. I was worried sick about Heath. I really love that jerk like a brother."

Despite her confusion, Helen couldn't resist a small chuckle. Agnes had finally admitted the affection she had for Heath. It was kind of cute that she'd waited so long when it was so damn obvious to everyone else.

"Anyway, he did it despite my freaking out. He went over to Derek's house. They played pool for freaking hours while I sat in a van with Nils practically chewing my nails off. But Heath was so good. He'd set up this whole story about getting dumped by a woman. They started on this misogynistic diatribe that naturally led Derek toward Jolie."

Helen's spine straightened. As much as she wanted to be free from suspicion, and even more important, she wanted justice for Jolie, it was still hard to hear the truth about her murder. "Okay. And Derek admitted he killed her?"

Agnes studied Helen's face. Her excitement dimmed as she realized the emotional impact this revelation had on Helen. "Yeah."

"Why? Why did he kill her?" Helen's voice broke as she asked. "Was it because of me?"

Agnes surged forward and wrapped her arms around Helen. "No, baby. No. That's not it."

Helen pulled away, forcing Agnes to look into her eyes. "Tell me what he said. Exactly. You heard it all, right?"

Agnes nodded. She bit her bottom lip as if she was contemplating not giving up the information. But Helen knew she would. So she just waited.

Agnes let out a deep breath. "He said Jolie was the one who wanted the divorce, not him. She'd gotten all her own money in the divorce and gave his trust fund back to his parents, which made him beholden to his mom and dad again. He was broke unless he did what he was told. But Derek was still in Jolie's will, and she hadn't changed her life insurance policies, yet. That money would mean freedom for Derek. It was only a matter of time before she changed all the documents and he lost his chance."

"So he planned it?"

Agnes nodded. "All of it. Turns out Erik, his golden boy younger brother—who I guess is the spitting image of Derek—was the other person the neighbor saw in the house. Derek was never supposed to be seen at the apartment, because Erik, who runs the family electronics business— that installed the system in that building—disabled the cameras at the condo. He left while Jolie was still alive and went to the bar, posing as Derek to give him an alibi during the time of the murder. It was all planned."

Helen fell into the cushions at her back. "Wow."

"I know...it's...a lot."

"It's exactly what I thought. But I never in a million years imagined it would actually come out like that...like...wow."

They sat in silence for a while. Helen stared at the ceiling and took a catalogue of her emotions. They were too convoluted and tangled to sort out and properly assess. That would take time. For now she needed to grieve.

"So..." Helen looked at Agnes again. "What happens now?"

"Heath is on his way to the police station with the tape."

"You didn't go with him?"

"No. I wanted to come home to you and tell you it's only a matter of time now and Derek will be arrested."

"So, that means..." Helen couldn't really say it.

Agnes placed her hands on Helen's cheeks. "It means, you're safe, my love."

****

Helen's apartment might have been in the quietest part of the city. Situated behind a large cliff and yet only steps away from a famous San Francisco street, it was as peaceful as it could get late at night.

Still, Agnes couldn't sleep. She stared at the window across from her. The early morning light was just beginning to break through the gauzy, fabric covering of the window. Behind her, Helen's warm body created the perfect spoon, cradling her in tenderness.

Agnes sighed. After all the worry, all the stress, things had worked out. With Helen free from suspicion, Agnes could help her grieve for Jolie. With Heath free from danger, Agnes could relax. And with Derek on his way to court, they could all turn their attention from solving the mystery to ensuring justice was done.

Despite all the work that lay ahead—both emotional and for her actual job—Agnes was more at ease than she'd ever been, because even as they'd slogged through the thick mud of the events over the past two months, she and Helen had found each other. And that, she knew, would change both their lives forever.

The sound of city traffic created a muted background that played mostly unnoticed as Agnes ruminated. But it was suddenly overshadowed by a loud thump.

The sound was impossibly close. Her brain scrambled to understand it as another sound followed on its heels. Behind her Helen stirred.

The balcony that sat off the living room had to be the source of the sound. Now it was clear the second noise was metal being pried, and a third, softer sound, was the glass door sliding open quickly, its frame hitting the other side with force.

Agnes shot up. Her feet swung from the bed. Before they touched ground a figure rushed through the bedroom doorway. Her heels had just slammed on the hardwood floor when Helen screamed. Agnes turned toward the danger. An ache exploded in the side of her head.

Everything went black.

Chapter Fifteen

There shouldn't be this much bumping. It felt more like a gravel road than the 101. The shocks must be bad. It was a strange thought to have for sure, but Helen's mind seemed to grasp onto details rather than focus on the big picture.

She couldn't see out the window of the SUV. She lay face down across the backseat, her arms tied in an awkward way from elbows to wrists with something harsh and scratchy. Twine maybe? An intense panic spread through her. Being unable to move her limbs immediately caused the need to be able to do so, and a form of rebellion took place inside her.

She tried to take her mind off her arms. That led to analysis of her sight, which consisted only of black leather. Despite not seeing the iconic red-orange towers, she could tell by the unmistakable sound of the textured road beneath the vehicle when they crossed the Golden Gate Bridge.

Helen shuddered. The image of Agnes—blood trickling down her temple, her body motionless on the bed—ran through her head again. She squeezed her eyes shut and tried to block it out. Derek had pulled her from the room at that point, one hand over her mouth, the other with a knife to her throat.

He tied her up good but didn't use a gag. Helen's muffled screams as Derek dragged her through the building to the street meant some neighbors must have heard. One door even began to crack open as the elevator doors shut behind them.

Kidnapping her from the fifth floor of an apartment building in the middle of the city was not exactly discreet. Meaning getting caught was no longer a concern to Derek. The idea flooded Helen's brain with implications.

Choosing to at least attempt to save herself, Helen asked, "Where are we going?" It was the first time she'd said anything coherent and direct to Derek since he'd shoved her in the back of the car and squealed away from her apartment complex.

She didn't expect an answer from him, and as the silence wore on, she gave up on getting one, instead focusing on direction as the car took a tight turn. They were barely into the North Bay. So if they were already getting off the freeway they were headed into the Marin Headlands.

Helen was lost in this internal compass when Derek spoke, his voice gruff and pained. "You know why I killed her?"

Heart clamoring in her chest, Helen shoved aside the horrific thought that *her* might mean Agnes and not Jolie. She took in as much air as she could with her chest pressing against the hard car seat and her arms wrenched behind her back. Her attempt to keep her voice steady failed, but she managed to get all her words out nonetheless. "I think you killed Jolie for money."

Derek laughed, the sound deeply terrifying. "That would be the easy answer wouldn't it? And it makes sense. But it wasn't what I was thinking about when I was squeezing my hands around her throat."

The ease with which Derek spoke about murdering Jolie struck Helen in the heart. The vibration from the impact pulsed through her chest and threatened to distract her from her plan to keep Derek talking and try to find a way out of this situation before it was her neck his hands were around. "So why?"

"I listened to this podcast recently." Derek's casual tone startled Helen again. "It was talking about the motives for murder. There's money, love, and pride, right?"

Helen's mind reeled. She'd listened to that podcast with Agnes while cooking dinner for a few nights in a row. Where was this going?

"You hear me?"

Helen pulled herself out of her confusion to focus on Derek. "Yeah."

"Okay, so. I could claim any of those reasons, right? Hell I could claim all three. But I've decided it was pride.

That bitch took the only thing I had left." Despite the quiet tone he began with, the heavy breaths he expelled after he finished speaking filled the car.

If the goal was to keep Derek calm, this conversation wasn't doing it. Helen tried to change the subject. "Where are we going?"

But rather than answer her question Derek asked a far more terrifying one. "You think I killed your girlfriend back there?"

A massive lump filled Helen's throat. She struggled to get her voice past it.

Again he was impatient with her slow response. "Well, do you?"

She finally managed to wheeze out an honest answer. "I hope not."

Derek laughed again. "I wasn't counting on her being there. I had to act fast. Grabbed some...shit I don't even know what it was...some fucking thing from your room and hit the shit out of her. She might be dead."

The terror and pain had to be pushed aside. There was no choice. Helen returned her focus to the road. They were moving slowly now. She shifted her head on the leather beneath her, trying to face the back of Derek's seat. "Where are we going?"

"It doesn't matter, does it?" The sudden defeat in Derek's voice signaled the worst possible outcome for them both. Defeat meant he didn't care what happened to himself. His sense of self-preservation was the one thing that might keep her alive long enough for someone to rescue her. "I know all about it. Some fucking setup by a fucking podcaster, of all things."

Helen's mind raced. Agnes had assured her that Derek didn't know about the sting. She'd also said he would be arrested before they even woke up this morning. But it was still dark when he'd dragged her to the car, the morning sun just now providing enough light for her to see the stitching on the seat beneath her chin. "What do you mean, setup?"

Derek slammed his hand on the steering wheel. "You motherfuckers all think I'm stupid. But I'm a smart motherfucker. I have friends everywhere, including at that stupid television station. My buddy is fucking anchor. That dumb-ass Heath didn't know that as soon as he got his fucking scoop, and the word spread to my buddy, I'd find out what he did. I got the fuck out of my house just before the cops got there. Shit, I saw them pull up in my rearview mirror." He cackled with pride.

Since Derek had been tipped off, what did that mean for her? "So why kidnap me?"

"You're my ticket to getting my name cleared, sweetheart. I'm going to use the media in my favor."

Helen didn't exactly know what Derek meant by this. But she rationalized that it could somehow keep her alive, at least for a while. "I know a back way out of the Headlands," she said. "We could head north and disappear on back roads."

****

Pain and fear rushed through every atom of Agnes at the exact moment she regained consciousness. Even before she opened her eyes, she stretched out her fingers in search of Helen. The sheets were too rough, the edge of the bed too close, and the plastic cord under her palm all wrong.

"Agnes. Agnes. Can you hear me?"

She wrenched open her eyelids to take in the sight of a ragged and desperate-looking Heath.

"Oh my God! Hi!" he said.

Agnes worked her throat for a moment before pushing out words. "Where's Helen?"

Heath's overexaggerated frown did nothing to soothe the terror flowing through her. "We're not sure."

Agnes leaned forward, desperate to sit up, but her body rebelled. She fell onto the hard mattress, and her head throbbed as it hit the pillow.

"You gotta take it easy, Agnes. The doctors say you suffered a pretty bad blow to the head." Heath's eyes roamed over her skull. As his head tipped to the side, a piercing blade of fluorescent light stabbed her eyes.

"How long have I been here? How long has Helen been gone?"

Heath pulled his phone from a cargo pocket on his shorts and glanced at it quickly. "It's three in the afternoon. It was around five a.m. that I got here, so..."

Agnes let out a heavy breath. Her head pounded in response. "Tell me everything you know."

Heath plunked onto a chair beside the bed. "Are you sure we should do that right now? I mean, you just woke up after like ten hours. Shouldn't a doctor check you out first?" His eyes shifted to the wooden door across the room.

"In a minute. Tell me first."

Heath ran a hand over his stubbled chin. "So, it was after two in the morning by the time Nils and I got to the police station and then we had to wait for Detective Poll, who was at home sleeping. Anyway, we all listened to the tape of Derek and me, and that took awhile. Then they waited for the warrant. The bottom line is the detective and a bunch of cops left to arrest Derek at like six or so. One of the cops who went along was Nils's brother-in-law, Jeff, you remember him? Anyway, Nils hops in the cruiser with him, and I went home to go to sleep. I'm not gonna lie. I was freaking exhausted. But as soon as I got home, Nils is calling me saying that Derek wasn't at his house when they went to arrest him. And like a second later, he's frantic and saying that neighbors reported a kidnapping at Helen's apartment building and I heard all these sirens and he's shouting that they're on the way to check on Helen. It was crazy."

Agnes swallowed hard. "What happened next?"

"The next call I got was from Nils telling me to come to the hospital. He said you were found unconscious and they were transporting you here. I wanted to be here when you woke up." He gave her a wry smile. "Took you long enough."

"Helen?"

"They're still looking. Nils went home, but he's in contact, you know. Plus everyone on the show is on it, too. Have been from the beginning. We'll find her."

Agnes's eyelids fell closed. She reveled in that darkness and wished it could take her away from this horrific fear and pain.

****

Going home should have been a welcome relief. Instead it was a painful reminder that nearly three whole days had gone by without a single hint as to where Helen was or what happened to her. Agnes was in living hell.

Heath, her constant companion, had trotted off to her shower on her insistence while she shuffled around the kitchen searching for something to eat, which was hard as hell to do since the thought of engaging in normal activities like eating and sleeping made her ill.

The dogs were still at the boarding facility. Agnes stared at their empty beds. She was pulled from the numbness by the sound of a popular eighties tune exploding from her pocket. That ringtone, assigned exclusively to Nils, had been an inviting constant in the last couple of days. He checked in every few hours with an update. Nils had worked harder than anyone to try to find Helen. Along with his brother-in-law and all the other friends they'd made at SFPD, he and the entire *True Crime Tonight* Crew were busting their asses to get her girlfriend back.

"Hey, Nils."

"Not him." The voice on the phone created an instant storm of terror that ripped through Agnes. She stared at the screen. Nils's grumpy "I have a deadline" face stared back at her. But this definitely wasn't Nils.

"Derek."

"That's right, Agnes. It's me."

"Where's Helen?"

His sinister cackle provided no comfort. "She's alive. She's here with me."

"Prove it."

"Now don't get ahead of yourself, sweetie. One thing at a time."

Derek had never struck Agnes as very bright. But his

calculating and confident tone betrayed that. Either he was far smarter than everyone made him out to be, or he was taking direction from someone else. That someone else couldn't be his brother, who currently sat in jail in between interrogation sessions from Detective Poll.

"Okay. What do you want?"

"Some things are about to happen, and I want you to go along with them."

Confusion almost eclipsed the fear as Agnes tried to understand his words. "What are you talking about?"

"Things are going to happen on your show. I want you to let them happen."

"What things?"

Derek let out a heavy breath. "Listen, just stay out of the way and Helen won't get hurt."

Somehow Agnes managed to force out a demand. "Let me talk to her."

A painful pause rang through the phone line. Then she heard it. "Agnes."

"Oh my God, Helen! Helen!"

But Helen's soft voice was replaced by Derek's. "Okay, so listen. Just go along with whatever happens on the air."

Agnes's brain screamed to catch up. What did *True Crime Tonight* have to do with Helen? Then another fear fought its way to the surface. Maybe Helen wasn't Derek's only victim. "Where's Nils?"

"Who the hell knows? You think I have to actually have his phone to make you think he's calling?"

She did think that. But apparently she was wrong. Heath would be able to explain. The important thing was she didn't have a second kidnapping victim on her hands. "Can I talk to Helen again?"

Derek didn't answer. He just hung up, leaving Agnes to collapse against her kitchen counter, tears no longer held at bay.

****

"You did the right thing coming to me." Detective

Poll's calm voice allowed Agnes to unclench her jaw for the first time since the phone call from Derek.

"I just don't want to do anything that will get Helen hurt."

Nils, in an uncharacteristically intimate gesture, reached over and squeezed her hand. "The police are going to help, Agnes."

Detective Poll leaned over the conference table. His grey suit, so out of place in the casual environment of the station's offices, crinkled as it touched the edge. "We have some new information that, combined with the phone call you got, is starting to put things into place for me."

Agnes's heart pounded. "What things? What information?"

Detective Poll folded his hands and looked over at Detective Hillman. The woman's icy expression seemed disjointed with the soft smile on her lips. "I've been spending a lot of time surveilling the Green family. They've been on the phone with Derek."

Agnes nearly jumped out of her seat. "What? Do you know where they are?"

Detective Hillman shook her head. "No. But we know that Derek's father has an insider at this show."

Nils and Agnes stared into each other's eyes. Agnes's pulse raced, but she was unable to speak. Nils didn't suffer the same affliction. "Inside my show? What are you talking about?"

Detective Poll launched into an explanation. "The Green's are rich. And a few generations ago, respectable. But Derek's father walks a fine line. He's been celebrated for his gifts to charity, but he's been in trouble with the law for illegal gambling activities. He's used to paying his way out of trouble. We suspect he plans to do the same for his sons."

"With someone from my show?" Nils tapped his chest in anger.

Detective Poll nodded.

Nils turned to Hillman. "Who? Tell me."

She shook her head. "I don't know exactly who. I only know they work at the show. And there's a plan to imply, live on the air, that Derek is innocent and Helen is guilty."

Nils's anger was barely contained. "How the hell would they do that right under my nose?"

In another odd movement, Detective Hillman shrugged. "I've thought a lot about this. They didn't give any details on the calls. But I'm thinking maybe one of the techs is planning to put something on the screen without your knowledge. Would that be possible?"

"No." Nils's nostrils flared.

"Maybe," Agnes said.

Nils stared at her, but Agnes kept her gaze across the table at the detectives. "A live show has a lot of moving parts. We rely on everyone to do their job. Could they make a mistake? Yes. Last week we had the wrong picture projected during the wrong story. It was an amateurish error, but it happens to everyone, even us. Even bigger, more professional shows."

Nils chewed his lip and nodded. "If one of my crew was planning something, they might be able to pull it off because I trust them. But I can stop it now."

"No. Don't." Detective Poll's voice was as stern as Agnes had ever heard it. "Just as Derek said on the phone call, we need to let it happen."

"You want me to let my show be sabotaged?" Nils threw his hands in the air.

Detective Poll's infuriating calm returned. "We do. It's the best way to determine who on your staff is in Green's pocket."

"I can find that out myself. Give me a couple hours."

Detective Hillman held up her hand. "There's more." She let out a deep breath and exchanged a glance with Poll. He nodded. "We have reason to believe that Derek will be watching tonight's show. And if he's convinced that Helen has been thoroughly implicated, he'd be willing to turn himself in and talk to us."

Agnes couldn't believe her ears. "Do you think he'd really do that?"

"His dad has very expensive lawyers. He knows that with the right story, the right reasonable doubt, the lawyers might be able to get him off. He's been very clear in the phone calls that he and his wife don't think a life on the run is a viable option for Derek. And we think they want Erik off the hook more than Derek. That'll never happen with Derek on the run."

Agnes took three deep breaths. Silence fell over the room like a thick blanket. Then Nils broke it. "We'll do it. We'll do what it takes to get Helen back."

****

Agnes openly expressed skepticism about a lot of things. She wasn't sure if crystals or meditation or past lives were real. Her mother, who was into all those things, often told her that skepticism wasn't the right term. She called her a disbeliever. Agnes supposed that was probably true. She tended to disbelieve many things until she could locate some solid, scientific proof.

Now, disbelief took on new meaning. It wasn't so much that she craved an explanation backed up by facts and statistics as she thought there was no way what was occurring right in front of her was actually happening.

"So, Jill, this story has really taken a twist," Kyle said. "The police went to arrest Derek Green, only to discover at his home evidence of his innocence."

Jill, seated at the anchor desk beside Kyle, was just as pale as Agnes felt. "His innocence, really?"

"Oh, yes. You see Derek and his brother, convinced that the police would never deliver justice for Jolie, had been investigating the murder on their own. And they turned up a whirlwind of evidence against the doctor."

Jill's bright-blue eyes pierced him. "What?"

Nils paced behind the engineer, Gale. "I can't fucking believe it's him."

Gale, who had no idea about the detectives' plot, turned her head to stare at him. "What?"

Nils pointed out the glass of the control room at the anchor desk. "He's in league with the fucking Greens. Of all the people."

Agnes didn't miss the expression painted across Gale's

face. It was something more than confusion or even surprise.

Outside the soundproof, glass-covered control room, the insanity continued. On the anchor set, Jill was in full defense mode. Also not in the loop, she attacked Kyle's logic. "Wait. Didn't he kidnap the doctor and nearly kill her girlfriend?"

Nils tore at his hair. "Fuck this. Go to commercial. I'm going to make him tell me the truth. Screw getting it out of him live on the air. This is stupid."

"But it's what Poll wanted." Agnes couldn't believe she was standing up for the public roasting of her kidnapped girlfriend. But there was more at stake than Helen's reputation. It was her life. "Don't put her in danger."

"She won't be, because I'm going to beat the location out of this idiot." Nils seethed. "Take it to commercial."

"I need another minute," Gale said.

That minute turned out to be a long one. Kyle, oblivious to Nils murderous plot against him, continued on. "Here's the real story, Jill. This innocent man has been accused of murdering his wife even though he has irrefutable evidence it was the doctor girlfriend. His brother gets tossed in jail, and he's on the run. Yes, he kidnapped the doctor. But that's because he wants to get her to confess, to straighten all this out."

"How do you know all this?" Jill asked.

Those were the last words heard before Gale managed to send the feed to a commercial.

While the television audience was escorted to a wheat-filled field to discover a new fragrance, back at the studio the entire crew swarmed Kyle. Nils reached him first. In a move that shocked everyone but the stoic Kyle, Nils grabbed him by the lapel and pushed him against the green screen at his back. "What the hell is going on?"

"I'm an investigative reporter. I've been investigating."

"Where the hell did you get this crazy shit from?"

Kyle's quirked mouth exposed his pure arrogance. "Don't you have a connection with the police, Nils? Ask them yourself about what they found in Derek Green's apartment."

Nils shook his head. Agnes mirrored the action, unable to do much more. Her anger and pain was too great to speak through, but Nils wasn't so paralyzed. "They found Jolie's diary with a bookmarked entry saying Dr. Nims had threatened her life. The handwriting expert took about thirty seconds to determine it was forged. How could you report that as real? What the hell?"

"I don't know that's it's forged. That's just one person's opinion."

Every mouth on the set dropped. Kyle had been a good anchor for the entire during his time on the show. Some people found him to be quick to anger, and of course, there were rumors of his gambling problem. But that hadn't ever affected his work. Now, on live television, Kyle was peddling an unfounded conspiracy against an innocent woman. It just didn't compute.

Jill, arms folded over her chest, hadn't moved from her spot at the anchor desk. "What about the rest?"

Kyle smirked. "I have a source."

"Oh we know," Nils said. "Derek Green's dad."

Kyle jerked his chin up and gazed at the ceiling, mouth sealed shut.

"It's true." Every pair of eyes turned to stare at Gale. "I dated this idiot for a while." She rolled her eyes. "As you all know. We went to a barbeque at the Greens once. Kyle and Derek's dad are super tight. Best friends since college. And of course, the Greens are loaded." She took a step toward Kyle. "I bet he offered to take care of all your debts and whatever you need after you get fired."

Kyle shrugged. "I was planning to retire anyway."

"So nothing to lose. Is that it?" Nils pushed his face toward Kyle. "No problem completely sacrificing your integrity and helping to turn public opinion on an innocent woman, who happens to be freaking kidnapped at the moment!"

Kyle pursed his lips and held his head up high. "I don't have anything more to say."

Nils turned to Agnes, his face pained and defeated. He opened his mouth, but she would never know what he planned to say because at that moment, Heath ran into the studio, hands held up over his head, wild expression pasted on his face. "Agnes! They found him!"

****

Helen twisted her hands in her lap to get some relief from the zip ties that had been her constant irritant for days. At least she'd convinced Derek to place her hands in front of her for their ride back to the Bay Area. The back of Derek's head blocked most of her view out the front window of the car, but she'd been able to watch the scenery go by as they traveled south.

Leaving behind the cabin had been a massive relief. Despite its ideal location nestled among the Redwoods, being trapped in the tiny one-room space with the man who murdered Jolie was a nightmare. The only point of light was when Derek called Agnes, allowing Helen the knowledge that Agnes was not only alive, but at home, answering her phone, talking.

"Where am I supposed to meet this cop?" Derek asked toward the phone hooked on his dashboard.

"The parade grounds at Fort Mason. He said it would be totally cleared out by the time you get there." Derek Green Senior's slightly scratchy voice had become a familiar sound to Helen over the last few days.

That she'd been able to listen in on all their conversations about the plan to clear Derek's name and thoroughly frame her for Jolie's murder wasn't comforting. It occurred to her more than once that it only made sense to be that transparent with her if Derek wasn't planning to keep her around.

"We're pulling up now. Is the show on yet?"

Helen let out a slow breath, careful not to make it audible. She could see the perimeter of police cars. Everywhere she looked, parked at a careful distance, a mix of police vehicles stood at the ready. Every one of them pointed directly at Derek's vehicle as it rolled down the street that ran along one side of the old fort's parade grounds. She had to get out of this alive now. She trusted that he couldn't kill her here, with all these police.

But Derek had no plans to leave the car just yet. He parked in the center of the road, leaned back in his seat, and pulled the phone off its holder. "Gotta go, Dad. I'll see you at the police station after."

"See you there, son. Enjoy the show."

As she had been doing for days, Helen stayed as still and silent as possible, allowing Derek to get caught up in his own world and take his focus off her and his unending anger about how things had turned out for him.

Derek mumbled, whether to her or himself Helen wasn't sure. "Time to see this shit go down." He held the screen up in front of the rearview mirror. "Can you see back there? Move to the middle."

Helen did as she was told, scooting to the center of the backseat so she could see the small screen. The theme for *True Crime Tonight* played as sinister scenes intertwined with opening credits ran across the screen, including Agnes's name, which brought Helen's heart into her throat.

As Derek and his father had predicted, the opening story was the drama of the Jolie Green murder and Helen's kidnapping. The anchor, Kyle, who was a friend in deep debt to Derek, Sr., did exactly as he promised. He presented, live on television, supposed evidence that Derek was innocent and that Helen was, in fact, the murderer.

Helen didn't really care if they slaughtered her name on live television. She wanted to get out of this car. She wanted her aching wrists free of the zip ties. She wanted Kimber's kisses on her chin. She wanted to hold Agnes in her arms again.

But all her desires careened out the window when the show abruptly went to commercial when Kyle was in the middle of roasting Helen and exonerating Derek.

Derek's rage always simmered just beneath the surface. During her time with him, Helen learned not to trigger it. The show's sudden break now lit a fuse leading straight to a shrapnel-filled bomb.

Derek dropped the phone on the passenger seat, and his

arm swung around. His fist landed on her right cheek. She reeled from the blow and her body fell over. Her head slammed onto the seat and everything went black.

****

The long, tortuous ride through the Marin Headlands ended, and Agnes saw a pool of cop cars surrounding Derek's black SUV. It stood still and ominously quiet.

The car sat there, engine running, only one head visible through the tinted windows. Agnes wrenched herself out of Nils's car and ran without caution toward Derek's lonely vehicle. A pair of arms wrapped around her waist. When her forward momentum suddenly stopped, she swung her legs out. But the arms held her steady until her feet were back under her.

Choppy breath hitched as she turned toward Detective Poll. "It's okay," he said.

"It's not okay! Where is she? Is she is even in there? What's going on?"

One hand firmly held her, and Poll pointed with the other. "Derek's on the phone with that man over there, who's a hostage negotiator. Helen's in the backseat. She's alive."

Agnes's eyes roamed Detective Poll's face and head. The small, plastic earbud stuck in his left ear was almost invisible. He cocked his head that way for a second, his attention on the man he'd pointed to before. But rather than look toward the stranger with the phone, Agnes swung her gaze back to the SUV. It was so still. Derek was so still. And she could see nothing in the backseat.

"I don't understand. How did you find them? Where have they been?"

Poll kept his eyes on the car as he spoke. "Derek's dad gave him up. We noticed a lot of bank activity from Mr. Green. Some of it involved the co-anchor of your show. When you told us about Derek's call, we put two and two together. We confronted Mr. Green and made a good case for charging him with aiding and abetting a fugitive. He finally gave it all up when we threatened to charge his wife, too, and throw them both in jail. He agreed to call Derek and tell him we believed his story, and that if he brought Helen in, we'd charge her with Jolie's murder, and he could make a deal for the kidnapping."

"He believed that?" Nils's voice came from behind Agnes, but she didn't bother to turn to look at him. She kept her gaze on Poll's calm face.

"His father was very convincing, and Derek agreed to meet us here. But he wanted to watch your show before he'd get out and talk. The kid truly believes his parents can bail him out of this. Combined with the media coverage saying he's innocent, he actually thought we'd arrest her and let him go."

"So why's he still in the car?" The sound of Nils's teeth grinding vibrated through Agnes. But details weren't important to her any more.

"When your show didn't come back on the air, and you went to a re-run, he panicked. He wanted to know why you stopped the broadcast. The negotiator's working on it." Detective Poll's voice was way too calm and even. Agnes could barely stand it.

Her own voice was high and laced with stress. "Where's Helen?"

Poll nodded toward the car. "In the backseat. The negotiator's trying to talk Derek into letting her out."

Agnes's breath was loud. The strong grip of Detective Poll on her shoulder, and the scent of the ocean somehow registered in her brain, slipping in around the stress and pain. She pinned her eyes on the grey window in the back of the car. A glint of sunshine struck the upper right corner of the glass and hit back at her like a laser beam, but she didn't look away.

Despite the sound of police officers shooing away spectators, overlaid by the shriek of gulls, it seemed as if time had stopped and the air hung heavy with stillness. Then the driver side door of the SUV cracked open. A hand pushed out between the door and the car frame, then a second hand appeared, both held wide open, fingers spread apart.

There was shouting, but Agnes wasn't able to discern one voice from another. A split second passed, then Derek was down, face first on the pavement. Moments later, an officer opened the back door of the car. He leaned over for a long, painful beat of time.

When the officer stood, Agnes pushed away from Detective Poll. She was in motion even as her eyes registered the body the officer pulled from the SUV.

It was Helen.

Chapter Sixteen

The blipping of the machine beside Agnes's ear lived in a space of twisted emotions. On the one hand, it was annoying as hell, counting off the time in excruciating detail. On the other hand, each beep meant Helen was alive.

If only Agnes could see her rich brown eyes open. She would give anything to gaze down on those beautiful lips moving, rather than still and quiet as they were now.

Helen's head injury wasn't serious. That's what the ER doctor had promised, backed up by Helen's boss and every person Helen worked with who'd made their way into her room to cry and smile at Agnes. Helen should wake up on her own at any time. That's what she'd been promised, again and again.

But the intense pull in her chest with each passing minute wasn't eased by reassurances. She needed Helen to open her eyes, to look at her, to speak to her, to hear Agnes say how much she needed her.

"Anything yet?"

Agnes ripped her gaze away from Helen. Heath's head poked into the room like a disembodied mirage.

Agnes managed a weak smile for him. "Nothing. Go home, Heath. I'm okay."

"Not going home. But I'll bring you something to eat. Wanna make a request?"

Agnes shook her head. She wasn't hungry, but she knew it didn't matter. Heath would bring her something and harass her until she shoved it down her throat.

"I'll be back." He disappeared and the door closed softly behind him.

Agnes turned back to Helen, ready to keep her vigil. But the closed eyelids she expected to find had been replaced by those dark-brown orbs she so longed to see.

"Helen." Breathy and shocked, her voice reflected her relief.

Helen took in an audible breath. When she let it out, her lips turned up just a tiny bit at the corners. "Hi."

A tear slipped down Agnes's cheek. "Hi."

Helen gazed slowly around the room. "Hospital?"

"Yeah. You got hit in the head."

Helen lifted her right hand to her temple. She lightly touched the bandage there, then she shifted her fingers across the small space between them and touched the bandage on Agnes's head. "Twins."

A second tear joined the first on Agnes's chin, where they dripped together onto the white hospital blanket covering Helen's chest. "Yeah. Twins."

"I was so worried about you."

Agnes snuffled. "Same here."

"So I guess Derek's in jail."

Agnes wiped the moisture off her chin. "Yeah. He sure is."

Helen expelled all her breath. Then slowly inhaled again. "Thank God for that."

Still trying to contain the tears that were coming down in full force, Agnes nodded. "You're safe now, baby. For real, this time."

Helen's hand slid down Agnes's cheek. "And so are you."

Agnes nodded again, unable to make words come. She knew there was something she'd planned to say the minute Helen opened her eyes. But she couldn't bring those words to the surface.

It was Helen who did it for her. "I love you."

Another round of tears flooded from Agnes's eyes. "Oh God." She pressed her forehead gingerly against Helen's. "I love you. So much."

****

A long day of surgery coupled with meetings and extensive charting left Helen drained. It had been thirteen hours since she left the little brownstone she now stepped back into. It was the sweetest place she'd ever had. Loath to go back to her apartment after all that happened there, she and Agnes found the perfect place to settle in. They'd only been here for six months now, but it was already home.

"Hey, you're home just in time," Agnes called from the kitchen.

Helen threw her backpack by the door, kicked off her shoes, and took a step onto the plush rug that ran across the hardwood floor from the foyer into the living space. She stood for a moment, reveling in the feel of her aching bare feet finally freed.

She padded down the carpet, following its flower pattern to the place where the living room met the kitchen. In a movement of habit, she slumped down onto a barstool at the island, propped her elbows on the countertop, and looked at the back of her lover.

Agnes's hair was getting long. She was trying to decide whether she wanted to cut it or let it grow even longer. But for now, it swung around, cascading over her shoulders and back as she lifted the lid of a pan, stirred something vigorously, then turned to a pot and did the same thing.

When she moved away from the stove and swiveled around, Helen had to catch her breath. This happened a lot. She was overcome, not just with Agnes's beauty, but also the realization that she was in Helen's life, hopefully forever.

"I'm just about done with dinner. I was hoping my timing was right." Agnes's radiant smile nearly knocked Helen off her stool.

"Sorry I'm late."

Agnes leaned over the counter and planted a sweet, soft kiss on Helen's lips. Then she slid a glass of red wine in front of her. "Long day?"

Helen nodded. "You?"

Agnes shrugged. "Not bad." She grinned.

Agnes was famous now. Not by sight—thank goodness—but by name. The podcast now named *Murder by the Bay,* had gone viral. She'd declined appearances on *True Crime Tonight,* instead choosing to remain behind the camera, but they were always sure to mention her name when she was responsible for a story, building on her fame. The bottom line was that Agnes seemed to enjoy her job more than ever before.

Helen said, "I was thinking."

Agnes leaned farther over the counter, her face just inches from Helen's. "Oh, yeah?"

"I was wondering if our jobs are too much for...for a family." The words nearly stuck in Helen's throat, but she forced them out.

At that moment, Jasper woke up and galumphed over to Helen to lick her calf. "You mean beyond him and Kimber?" Agnes asked, chuckling. The poodle peeked out from her small, round, fuzzy bed to stare at them both.

Helen scratched Jasper's ears. "Yes, like...like kids." She swallowed hard and took a long sip of her wine.

Agnes continued to smile, as if what Helen said wasn't completely out of the blue. "I've been thinking about that, too."

Helen slammed her stemless wineglass down on the counter, startling Jasper, who edged away to lie down on the rug. "You have?"

"Yeah." Agnes casually took a sip from Helen's glass. "I was thinking I could work from home. You know, making podcasts. I have two more lined up. I could quit the show and just focus on those."

Helen had a hard time speaking. Her mouth flopped uselessly. Which caused Agnes to laugh at her, of course, and say, "You look a little surprised, sweetheart. Did you think we were that far off?"

Helen managed to shake her head. "No...I just...no."

Agnes planted another soft kiss on Helen's lips, this one lingering. "I think we should talk about a family. I'll stay home, but either you're carrying or we're adopting. I'm not birthing anything."

Helen swallowed again, her heart so full she could barely breathe. "Okay. Let's adopt. I always wanted to do that."

"Okay."

"Just like that?"

"Not exactly." Agnes stood tall. She looked across the counter at Helen, her expression suddenly serious.

"No?"

"No. There is one condition to all this family business."

"Okay?"

"You have to marry me."

A tear fell from Helen's left eye and landed on her upper lip. "You bet I will."

THE END

About the Author

Benna Bos is an author, non-profit manager, and adjunct professor of Anthropology. Her greatest love is romance. Mixing Cozy Mystery with engaging love stories, Benna plays on her love of place and her obsession with true crime podcasts. San Francisco is the setting she is most obsessed with, and it happens to be her current home. Benna loves to read, write, play with her dog, and go on road trips.

Bringing LGBTQAI+ Stories to Life

Visit us at our website: www.flashpointpublications.com

CPSIA information can be obtained
at www.ICGtesting.com
Printed in the USA
FSHW020958061021
85226FS